AVALON
A SOOTHSAYER NOVELLA

ALLISON SIPE

LIKE MAGIC
STUDIO

❋ Created with Vellum

ALSO BY ALLISON SIPE

SOOTHSAYER SERIES

Soothsayer

Avalon: A Soothsayer Novella

Trivium

Le Fay: A Soothsayer Novella

Elysium

REALMS SAGA

Realm of Flames & Steel

Realm of Stars & Shadows

BOOK PLAYLIST

If you like to listen to music while you read, then you're in luck!
We've created a playlist just for Soothsayer on Spotify and you
can listen here:

To David, my editor.
Working with you has been a dream come true.
You so eloquently help me find the perfect words to tell my story.

*"Our deeds still travel with us from afar,
and what we have been makes us what we are."*
- George Eliot

DAY 1

My tires squealed against the pavement as I made a sharp right turn, racing toward the coast. I could feel Violet's heart starting to race as I floored the accelerator against the carpeted Tesla floor mat.

"Hold on, Violet. I'm coming," I said through gritted teeth.

My phone rang through the car speakers and I answered it on the first ring, effortlessly pressing the Bluetooth button on the steering wheel with my thumb. "Did you find her?" I asked, my words rushed and clipped.

"Yes. Bethany said she's being held on the beach at *Pacifica Pier*. Annabel is orbing us now," Brett, my ever-serious sister, said. Normally I'd find her militaristic no-nonsense attitude irritating, but things were different now that Violet's life was on the line.

"Okay, see you shortly." I took another corner faster than I should've.

"Robert, take a deep breath. We'll get her out of this." Brett did her best to sound reassuring.

"I'll breathe easy once Violet's safe." I pressed the end button on the screen and quickly typed Pacifica Pier into the navigation. I was fifteen minutes away. I could only hope I wouldn't be too late.

A searing pain shot through me from the bond. My vision blurred and I had to fight the throbbing radiating from my head. Gripping the steering wheel so tightly I thought it might snap, I took a deep breath, gathered my senses and accelerated forward.

I needed to get to Violet. Now.

Throwing the gearshift into park the second I arrived, I shoved the door open and sprinted toward the beach. With a quick jump over the railing, I landed on the rocks below and scanned the shoreline.

"Annabel, get her out of here!" I yelled over the din as my eyes caught Violet's for a brief moment. With the connection spell still active, I could feel her fear ripping through her like a jagged blade. The urge to run to her and shield her from any more pain propelled me forward.

Quickly I maneuvered across the beach, dodging Cinder orbs and fireballs. Someone released a Galvin spell and green tendrils of electricity crackled across the shore like tentacles, electrocuting anything they came in contact with and causing uncontrollable muscle spasms.

Annabel ran toward Violet, disappearing and reappearing at intervals, dodging both people and explosions as I took advantage of the fact that most of Aiden's people had their backs turned to me. Running up behind one of them, I quickly snapped his neck before taking my place next to Brett.

Another wave of Violet's emotions surged through me. I tried to push what she was feeling aside, but she was beginning to panic and the shock of it choked me and left me gasping for air. We needed to get her out of here before it was too late.

"Annabel!" I yelled again. She was the only one who could get Violet out of here quick enough to survive the firestorm of Magic around us.

"I can't!" she yelled back, "she's been anchored to this plane."

"Do something, we can't lose her!" I turned my head just in time to see a massive wall of fire barreling down on Brett and I. My shield materialized on instinct and stopped the flames from engulfing us. Brett dropped to her knees, dug her hands into the wet sand and summoned the ocean water, making it rise high above us and douse the blazing inferno battering against my shield.

"Stop her!" someone yelled. Searching the beach, I saw green sparks flying toward Annabel while she was mid-orb. Her body blinked for a moment, shimmering as she struggled to stay grounded and then reappeared as she fell to the sand, convulsing and screaming. I looked in the direction where the sparks were coming from and recognized Lila's sharp features and long blonde hair. A part of me hoped she wouldn't be here. Our history made things complicated, and even though I'd moved on, it would still pain me to kill her.

Running toward Annabel, I watched her writhe in the sand as the Galvin spell kept her pressed against the ground, when suddenly I found myself gasping for air. No matter how much oxygen I sucked into my lungs, I couldn't breathe. Looking toward the pier, searching for Violet, I realized she was under water. She was suffocating and I could feel the agony of her last breath burning in my own chest and throat. Looking back toward Annabel, I saw her take off toward Violet while Jake was busy fighting off Lila.

My feet tossed sand into the air as I ran toward Violet. The connection spell was getting stronger the more she struggled to survive. My vision blurred and my throat burned as I made my way across the shore.

A stout, portly man and a woman who was more limbs than body appeared in front of me out of thin air, blocking my path to Violet. I looked behind me to see if anyone else could get to her, but everyone was busy with their own fight. Brett stood in front of Lila and absorbed the woman's Galvin spell into her body. She was the only person I'd ever known who could withstand the effects of the spell. In fact, it seemed to make her stronger. Jake fought against two guys and Annabel rolled on the ground in a brawling struggle with a red-headed woman.

"Go help Violet!" Brett ordered at Annabel again.

My anger and Violet's terror surged through me with a force I'd never felt before. Every nerve in my body pulsed with an energy that begged to be released. The gangly woman ran at me as the man raised his hands above the sand, making each tiny pebble rise from the ground into a twister. I didn't have time for this. Each one of my muscles tensed and the rage pumping through my blood pulsed off of me in a circular formation, sending the two assailants flying backward. The sand twister crumbled, throwing grains of rock and seashells flying in all directions. Taking a fraction of a second to assess myself, I patted my torso. I'd never felt so much Magic course through me before.

My two opponents rebounded quickly and before I could take more than two steps, the woman stood blocking my way again while the stout man circled around me.

"You know what to do, Jo," the heavy man growled and the lanky woman smirked and nodded.

I looked between Jo and the pier to gauge the distance. Annabel had just orbed next to Violet with Taylor Deardon and they worked together to untie Violet from the pillar.

Another wave of energy burst out of me but this time they blocked the blow and threw two Cinder orbs my direction. I raised my shield just as the first one hit. It bounced off of me into one of their other men. He froze mid-run, then disintegrated into a pile of ash.

Jo's unnaturally long fingers held her cheeks as she screamed like a wolf in pain. Arms flailing, she made a run for me again. Her partner vanished into thin air, and I knew I needed to keep my guard up. She jumped into a spin-kick formation and I ducked out of the way just in time. Landing gracefully back on her feet, I caught her by the waist and tackled her to the ground. A ball of Arcane Magic formed on my palm, ready to take her out when I fell forward with someone on my back. Jo disappeared from underneath me and the Arcane orb in my hand reabsorbed into my palm. Snarling at my missed opportunity, I grabbed the guy on my back and threw him over my shoulder. He landed in the shallows with an audible *thud.*

Violet's emotions gripped me again and I doubled over in pain. The air in my lungs burned in concert with Violet's agony. A thousand tiny knives pricked over my skin, forcing another uncontrollable pulse of energy to erupt out of me. The dark-haired man I'd thrown over my shoulder flew backward as the pulse of Magic hit his body.

"Annabel," Jake's voice tore across the shore with an edge of urgency.

Looking in Annabel's direction, a stream of Devil's Flame licked across the beach, aiming directly for her. Blinding yellow light moved unnaturally, changing directions on a whim and hitting the pillar Violet was strapped to. Annabel and Taylor quickly jumped out of the way, diving into the ocean and out of sight.

Enough was enough, I put up my shield and made a beeline for Violet. Nothing would stop me from reaching her this time. The cold water stung my legs as I rushed into the surf. The pain in my chest grew the closer I got to her and I had to fight against the overwhelming surge of terror, panic, and anguish coursing through me from the binding spell.

About fifty yards away, I dove into the waste-deep water and began to swim. When I reached the pillar, I took a deep breath and submerged myself. My hands fell on Violet's shoulders and I quickly found her mouth. Pinching her nose, I placed my mouth on hers. She tensed for a moment and then seemed to understand what I was trying to do. Relaxing against my lips, she let me blow air into her mouth.

Another wave roared above us, and I knew that she would die if we didn't get her out of the water soon.

The pillar Violet was tied to vibrated as the battle for her life waged on above us. I squeezed her shoulder for reassurance and then resurfaced.

"Robert, give her this," Annabel said. She threw an oxygen tank and mouthpiece to me. I grabbed it, gave her a quick nod of thanks, and took another deep breath before dunking back below the water line.

I felt around for Violet's shoulders again and found her body limp under my hands as I placed the mouthpiece between her lips. I put my hand on her chest and gently pushed, telling her to breathe, but she didn't move.

Resurfacing, I yelled at Taylor and Annabel, "Get her out of here, she's dying."

"We're trying!" Annabel snapped back. "We just need one more minute."

"Get back to the fight, they need you," Taylor yelled over the rumble of the ocean as he worked on the ropes tying Violet to this plane.

As I pushed through the water, I made a run toward Lila and her companion.

With his back turned toward me, I knew I had a clean shot. Summoning a stunning orb, I aimed it at the center of his spine. The orange orb flew across the beach as I ran toward them, but he turned just in time to deflect the spell. His maneuver, however, allowed me to close the gap and land a clean punch to his jaw. His face swept to the side and then he was back on me in the blink of an eye. A black orb appeared in his hand and I threw up my shield. Instead of throwing the sphere as I expected, he held the ball of Magic against my shield and stared at me with eyes like death.

My defense crackled under the pressure and darkness spread out from the orb like tentacles where it touched my shield. I couldn't hold the Cinder spell at bay much longer, so I took a gamble. Retracting my Magic, I let my only defense shimmer away, as I ducked down and swung my leg out to throw him off balance.

He fell to the ground and the Cinder orb disappeared.

I gathered my fist to take another swing at him, but he jumped up and stepped back toward Lila.

It was then that I realized a bright light was glowing just behind me. Looking over my shoulder at the source of the light, I saw Brett glowing like the sun, brilliant and terrifying. Lightning erupted from her outstretched arms and crackled down her entire body.

Lila and the man I'd just been fighting turned their attention toward Brett. *That's not good,* I thought. I ran in front of my sister and summoned my shield just as Lila's spell flew at us.

The force of it knocked the wind out of me and I fell to the ground.

"We need to make sure Robert comes with us!" Lila yelled over the roar of the battle.

A few of Lila's henchmen shimmered and disappeared. They were retreating.

Brett swung her arms open and then brought them together as forcefully as she could, sending our attackers flying as a stream of raw electricity arced into each of them.

"Are you okay?" Brett asked as she knelt next to me.

"I'm fine, get Violet." I winced as I got to my feet.

Brett nodded and ran toward the pier where everyone was gathering to help Violet. As she did, Lila approached me with arms raised in surrender while I dusted the sand off of my jeans.

"Lila," I said through gritted teeth.

"It's nice to see you again, Robert." A wicked smile spread across her face.

In one quick motion, she reached out to me, bound my wrist and said a spell under her breath. The ground disappeared beneath me as the world swirled around me in an array of colors.

A moment later, my legs hit something solid and gave out beneath me. I lay still for a moment to catch my breath before opening my eyes. We weren't on the beach anymore, that much I knew. I could feel it in the air.

Rolling onto my side, I pushed myself up and healed all of my wounds. Then I scanned the area, looking for any sign of a threat, but it was just the three of us.

We had landed on an unnaturally green lawn that had been manicured to perfection. A large stone estate loomed to the right of us, just out of reach of the tree line. Seagulls squawked overhead as dark, ominous clouds pressed down on us, promising rain.

We must be close to the sea, I thought as I watched a few of the seagulls land on the grass nearby. That was a start. At least there might be boats nearby I could use to escape. Still, I couldn't shake the feeling that we had come a very long way from the California coast. There was something familiar about the cold, humid air, but I couldn't quite put my finger on what it was.

"Let's go. He'll be waiting for us," Lila said, starting toward the estate.

I took a hesitant step forward. I could make a run for it, but where would I go? I had no idea where I was or where I could find help.

"Ian," Lila snapped at him, "Will you please." She smiled and motioned toward me.

Ian shoved me by the shoulder and I resigned myself to getting more information before trying to escape.

As we approached the estate, an older gentleman emerged, meeting us at the front of the property.

"We have a present for you," Lila announced, her deep voice purring with affection.

Ian walked alongside me, looking utterly dejected. I wondered idly what could've made him so distraught. Violet was struggling for her life on the beach and they had me prisoner. What more could he want?

"Is The Waker dead?" the older gentleman asked. He folded his arms across his chest as we came to a stop in front of him. His slender build did nothing to detract from the unspoken authority emanating off of his presence as his eyes narrowed in an appraising gaze.

"Of course. We performed the ritual like you said and stole their Healer just to be safe." Lila's voice cracked when she used my moniker instead of my name.

Ian shoved me down on my knees as realization began to set in as to who this man was. A small tremor of fear settled in the pit of my stomach and I prayed I was wrong.

"Very nice." He eyed me up and down. "But what am I supposed to do with him?" He looked at Lila in disgust. Out of the corner of my eye, I saw Ian smile as he shifted back and forth from one foot to the other in a nervous little dance.

"I thought you'd be happy, Father," Lila said. Her voice still held an edge of pride, but she wrung her hands together with a child-like worry.

My instincts were correct. The old man was the infamous Aiden Partridge. I looked him over more carefully and measured him against every horror story I'd ever heard. He wasn't what I pictured, but he was cold and stiff as if his heart had truly frozen over.

"You're sure she's dead?" Aiden asked, addressing Ian this time.

"I wouldn't be here if I thought she was alive," he said with pride. I wanted to punch my fist through someone's skull. How could they speak so casually about someone's death? The hope that Brett and the others had found a way to save her was the only thing keeping me from lunging at Aiden in a suicidal rage. I tried to reach out through the Connection spell but felt nothing. Ice froze my heart and I rationalized that I must be too far away from her to feel anything. But deep down, I knew the spell wasn't hindered by distance.

I glared at Aiden with utter disdain and spat at his feet. "Such a big man you are, having your daughter do your dirty work," I said through gritted teeth.

"How dare you speak to-" Ian erupted, but Aiden cut him off with a simple, silencing raise of his hand.

Aiden knelt down in front of me, grabbed my face between his thumb and finger and forced me to look him full in the eye, "It must be difficult to know that you failed not only Violet, but your destiny," he chided with a wry grin.

I tried to pull my head free, but he tightened his grip and leaned in closer. "Robert must find her before it's too late," he whispered and let go of my face.

Those were Belinda's words to William. I was the one who was meant to find Violet. I was the one who was meant to protect her. But how could he possibly know that? William was the only one Belinda told that night. Only another Soothsayer would know what Belinda shared with William, but how could any Soothsayer betray their gift and work with Aiden?

Aiden rose to his feet and looked me over once more. "Throw him in one of the cells for now. I'm sure we can find some use for him." He turned on his heel and walked back the way he'd come.

Lila followed after her father and they disappeared inside.

"Get up." Ian kicked me with his thick, leather boot.

We trudged across the lawn to the back of the house. There we came across a set of double doors in the ground, like a tornado shelter or an old root cellar. Ian pulled one of the doors open and pushed me down the stairs. We passed a few empty cells as we made our way down the concrete path. One cell, second to last on my left, held an older woman who had honestly seen better days. A plastic tray holding a sandwich and a bottle of water sat on the floor of her cell, untouched. Her eyes tracked me as we passed and her mouth parted slightly as if she wanted to say something but thought better of it.

We arrived at the furthest cell from the entrance. Ian slid the bars open and shoved me inside. Following me into the cell, he slammed the bars closed behind him and waved his hand over the lock. An electric blue force field shimmered across the metal, and suddenly I felt empty.

"Healers, always thinking you're so much better than the rest of us." Ian fumed and punched me square in the stomach.

I coughed and doubled over. With my hands still bound, I couldn't defend myself. Looking inward, I tried to summon my shield but found nothing. My Magic was gone. But how?

Ian chuckled and said, "Did you really think we wouldn't take precautions?" He tapped the bars with his knuckles and the force field rippled across my prison.

"What purpose can you possibly have for keeping me here?" I asked as I righted myself.

"I was wondering the same thing." Ian's voice held an edge of jealousy as he took a step toward me. He didn't want me here, that much was clear, and the way he looked at Lila when she wasn't watching made me wonder.

"You're upset Lila brought me here at all, aren't you?" I guessed.

"Don't you dare speak to me about Lila." Ian shot toward me and grabbed my shirt in his fist.

I laughed. "Do you really think you have a chance with her?"

"I'm warning you." He clenched his jaw and balled his other hand into a fist.

I looked him up and down and said, "You're not really her type, trust me," I paused and looked him straight in the eye, "I would know."

Ian swung at me, his fist landing right on the bridge of my nose. A loud crack and an explosion of pain radiated from the center of my face. Blood sprayed from my nose and dripped at a steady pace. Ian reached back to punch me again, but I threw my weight against him and caught him off-guard. Dodging to the right and then left, I quickly got behind him and threw my bound arms over his head. Getting his thick neck in the crook of my arm, I pulled tight, cutting off his airway. His elbow shot backward into my torso and knocked the wind out of me. My grip loosened and he reached around, grabbing the back of my shirt and throwing me over his shoulder. Landing on the cold, hard cement, I struggled to breathe. Before I could right myself, Ian was on top of me. His fists came at me with a one-two punch as I rolled him off of me in one quick motion.

A dark chuckle escaped my throat as I rose to my feet and said, "She doesn't even notice you, does she?" I spat a mouthful of blood to the floor. I knew I shouldn't goad him, but I needed a way to release everything I was feeling. Anger, fear, anxiety, they all clawed at me and propelled me forward.

Ian lunged at me again, but I quickly dodged out of the way.

"After everything you've done for her, she still doesn't even take a second glance at you," I cackled.

"That's enough!" he yelled and closed the gap between us in two strides.

"It must be so hard knowing that some of us don't even have to try to get her attention." I shrugged and pain shot down my left side.

He punched me across the jaw and grabbed me by the shirt again. His face was only a couple inches from mine, his breath warm on my face as dark amusement glistened in his eyes. The *click* of a switchblade being opened caught my attention and I shook my head in disapproval.

"You can't kill me. Aiden wants me alive," I said through bloody teeth. My mouth tasted like salty pennies as blood dribbled down the back of my throat.

"For now. But I will be the one to kill you when the time comes." His fist connected with my stomach again and I sunk to the floor. My body throbbed in cadence with Ian's footsteps as he stepped away from me.

"Pathetic," Ian scoffed as he unlocked my cell.

"Give Lila my best." I struggled to get the words out as I stood up.

"Don't push me, *Healer.*" His head twitched to the side as the bars slid closed in front of me.

"You think I'm afraid of you?" A short, dark laugh escaped my throat. "I have nothing left to lose." I held his eyes. It was true. If Violet really was dead, then my entire life had been a waste.

"You always have something to lose." A wry smile spread across his face as he waved his hand again and my wrists fell free from their shackles.

Without another word, that sick smile still plastered on his face, Ian left.

He really was unhinged. I realized it was only a matter of time before Aiden lost his hold over him, and I sure as hell didn't want to be around when he did.

"You should be careful what you tinker with. The puzzle pieces don't quite fit together if you know what I mean," the old woman said and nodded in the direction Ian had just exited.

"I'll keep that in mind," I replied and smiled as kindly as I could manage given the circumstances.

Pulling my shirt over my head and using it as a rag, I wiped as much of the blood off of my face as I could. I tried to tap into my Magic again to heal myself, but nothing happened. I felt empty and naked without my Magic. It felt wrong to feel so normal. And for the first time, I finally understood how Violet must have felt when she first got her Magic. Being normal now, I realized how different having Magic felt.

"Oh Violet," I said under my breath. I needed to find a way out so I could get back to her. I wouldn't believe she was dead. Our souls were connected, after all. Wouldn't I be able to feel it if she was really gone? There had to be some way for me to reach out to her and make sure she was alright. I sat down on the edge of the two-inch thick mattress and closed my eyes. I focused my energy inward, hoping I could feel something or get a sense of what she was feeling.

"If you keep concentrating that hard you might lay an egg," the old woman said, breaking my concentration.

I sighed. As much as I wanted to believe I could still feel Violet through our connection, I knew it wasn't possible if I couldn't use Magic.

"I just wish I knew for sure that she was alright," I admitted without looking up.

"Of course she is, dear. It's going to take a lot more than a little spell to kill The Waker," the old woman said with a light chuckle.

I raised my head then. "You mean you can see her? Violet, she's alive?" Hope sprung up inside me as I pictured Violet unharmed and safe. I crossed the small space to the metal bars in three strides and searched for the old woman's face hidden in the shadows.

"She's alive," the woman said with a warm smile.

I breathed a sigh of relief. "You're a Soothsayer then?"

"Once I went by that title, but *he's* made a disgrace out of my gift. It's nothing but a curse now." She looked up at the ceiling, toward the house above us.

So that's how Aiden was able to quote Belinda's words, I thought as I looked her over carefully.

"Why serve him at all?" My broken nose made my voice sound stuffy and I cringed at the thought of having to pop it back into place.

"I don't have a choice." She shook her head as a shadow crept into her eyes.

"How long have you been down here?" I reached my arms through the bars and let them rest on the cool metal.

"Too many sunsets to count." She sighed and looked up at the small window above her head.

"I didn't catch your name. I'm Robert."

"Clara." The old Soothsayer placed her hand against her chest and inclined her head. "And I know who you are, Mr. Maxwell. I've had many visions of you."

I looked away, suddenly self-conscious. It was always an odd experience interacting with a Soothsayer. They seemed to know more about you than you knew about yourself.

"You must get back to Violet, no matter what the cost," she continued, catching my eyes. "She cannot succeed without you." She nodded, having said what she needed to say, then turned away from me and sat back down on her bed.

I wanted to ask her a million questions, but it was clear she was dismissing me. Leaving her to her own devices, I tried to get comfortable on the sorry excuse for a mattress and stretched my legs.

Now that I was alone with my thoughts, I let them drift to Violet. Guilt raked through me as I pictured her helpless on the beach. There was no way I'd ever be able to forgive myself for not getting to her sooner. I was supposed to protect her, keep her safe, and I'd failed her again. Living through her terror as she was taken from the cabin in Yosemite had been my own personal hell. It didn't matter that Lila had sent a squad of men to keep me occupied while they ran off with her. I never should've left her side. I wanted to show her she could still have a normal life with normal friends, but that was foolish, and I knew better. I let my feelings for her cloud my judgment.

Once I get out of here, I swore to myself, I'll never leave her side again.

It wasn't going to be easy to escape without Magic, but I had to find a way. If only I could get close to Lila, I might be able to use my history with her to my advantage. She may not be the young schoolgirl I once cared for, but I knew who she was underneath all her bravado.

Granted, getting close to her was the last thing I wanted to do. I wanted to kill her for even laying a finger on Violet. But again, it was my fault she ended up here, back under her father's thumb. If I hadn't left things so badly with her, then maybe she wouldn't have crawled back to Aiden. I would have to tread very lightly if I was going to pull this off.

Exhaustion from the battle began to creep across my eyes, but there was something I had to do before I fell asleep. Thankfully, I'd observed my instructor perform this task a hundred times when he thought someone deserved to feel the pain of a broken nose rather than just heal it with Magic. This was going to be unpleasant.

Taking a few deep breaths, I put my fingers on each side of my nose and snapped it back into place. Ripples of pain radiated across my face and hammered behind my eyes. I tried to breathe through my nose, but it was too swollen for any air to pass through. *My throat's going to be dry in the morning,* I thought as I closed my eyes and settled into my temporary quarters.

DAY 2

I had no idea what time it was, or how long I'd slept. Early morning sunlight pooled on the floor through the tiny slats high above my cell. Clara, the Soothsayer, snored peacefully across the hall as I stared at the smooth, gray ceiling. The sound of a heavy metal door creaked open and slammed shut with a *bang*.

This is going to be an unpleasant morning, I thought.

Angry footsteps slapped against the concrete floor, advancing toward me as I held onto the last few moments of peace I would have.

The bars to my cell screamed in protest as they slid open and a heavy boot stepped inside my prison. A Magical force lifted me from the bed and tossed me across the small space like a rag doll. My back cracked against the bars and I slumped to the floor with a heavy groan. I guessed the force field preventing Magic was down. As I lifted myself onto my hands and knees, a worn brown boot swung toward my face. I grabbed the boot before it could connect with my jaw as an angry grumble exploded above me.

"How'd they do it?" Lila yelled and kicked her leg free of my grasp.

"How did who do what?" I slowly and carefully got to my feet.

My body ached all over from the beating I'd taken yesterday. I tried to heal myself now that the barrier was down, but before I could tap into my Magic, Lila raised the shimmering blue force field back into place.

"Don't play games with me, Robert. How did they save Violet?" Lila asked, a threat implied in her voice.

I smiled and said, "Oh, is she alive then?" Even though Clara had confirmed yesterday that Violet was alive, it was still gratifying hearing directly from Lila that they had failed.

"She won't be for long. When my father learned she survived, he decided to take matters into his own hands."

"Is that right?" I rubbed the kink in my neck and bit back the pain. "So what, he thinks he'll be able to kill Violet when everyone else has failed?"

"He can and he will." She took a step toward me, closing the gap between us. "Now tell me how they did it." I could feel her breath on my face as she sneered at me.

"I wouldn't know, would I?" I leaned back against the cement wall and crossed my arms. "I've been locked up in here." I raised my hands and looked around to further illustrate my point. I couldn't help feeling smug, knowing Violet was still alive.

"You think this is funny?" Lila asked. Her eyes bulged out of her head and the dark circles under her eyes indicated she hadn't gotten much sleep the previous night. She had always been irrational when she was tired, and I was never very tolerant of her mood swings.

"It's a bit amusing that you keep failing to kill a woman who barely even believes in Magic, let alone knows how to use it," I noted with a wry grin.

She swung in an attempt to punch me, but I caught her wrist and pulled her off-balance.

She twisted her wrist free and kicked at my shin. "You don't get it, do you," she scolded. "She's going to destroy the Magical world by waking The Lady. How can you protect her?"

"Destroy the Magical world? Lila, can you really be so naïve?" I stared at her in disbelief as a pang of sadness ran through me. Had Aiden really warped her into thinking Violet was the evil one?

"I'm not naïve, Robert, I'm just not afraid of the truth." She turned her back to me and took a few steps away.

"And what truth is that?" I asked. A sarcastic laugh escaped my throat as I leaned against the cement wall.

Lila paused and looked at me over her shoulder, her blonde hair falling like a curtain and shielding half her face. "That Violet will wake The Lady and force the Magical world into subjugation." The fury in her eyes told me she truly did believe Violet was the evil one.

"That's bullshit and you know it. You've heard the prophecy, we all have. The only reason she'll wake The Lady is to stop Morgana." I ran my hand through my hair and pushed myself off the wall, frustrated. "And I'll give you one guess as to who's trying to bring that evil witch back from beyond the veil."

Recognition flashed across her eyes, but she shook her head and yelled, "You're wrong!" She snapped at me.

"Am I?" I stepped towards her, adrenaline pumping through my veins as I stared into her cold blue eyes. "Then why have so many Magical people been murdered over the last few years with the same symbol you carved into Violet?" My voice reverberated off the concrete walls and my hands shook as I tried to keep my anger and disgust under control.

Lila only shook her head, as if she were turning her eyes from the truth. "She's played you, Robert, can't you see that? Or are your rose-colored glasses too thick to see the truth?" She shoved me hard and I took a step back, stunned.

Her head cocked to the side and she looked at me like a spider inspecting a fly in its web. "Oh, did you think your little tryst was a secret?" She cooed. A low chuckle emanated from her chest. "I thought you were supposed to protect her, not seduce her."

She was right. I *was* supposed to protect her, but I'd let my feelings cloud my judgment.

"How I may or may not feel has nothing to do with the fact that your father is systematically taking out anyone who can put a stop to his rise in power," I said, taking a deep breath to steady the anger building in my chest as I stepped toward her. "He's using Dark Magic to do it. You and I both know that performing rituals is forbidden."

"It was forbidden centuries ago, things change," Lila informed me as she moved the bars aside and stepped out of my cell, keeping her back to me.

"Listen to yourself. The woman I knew would never let herself be caught up in Dark Magic. You think what you're doing doesn't have consequences? Of anyone, I'd think you'd know better."

"That's enough." Her voice echoing off of the cement walls as she spun around to face me.

But I wasn't done with her. I'd poked at her moral compass, reminded her of the past, but now it was time to plant the seeds of doubt and make her question Aiden's actions.

"If your father really is the good guy, then why is he searching for The Pieces of Three?" I asked, slowly and deliberately walking toward her.

Lila's bottom lip fell open. "Pieces of Three?" she asked and the hatred in her eyes soften as her brow furrowed in confusion.

I leaned against the metal barrier and said, "Ahh, so he hasn't told you everything then, has he?" *Gotcha.*

She huffed and shook her head. "You really think it's that easy to get into my head?"

I wrapped my fingers around the bars and smirked at her unease. "I know it is."

She blinked twice and took a step back. "Things were different back then. I've changed and clearly so have you." She looked me up and down.

"True, I've grown and changed, but my morals and principals are still the same. I can't say the same for you though. The girl I knew never would've killed someone just for daddy's approval."

She scowled hard enough I could have sworn she wanted to throw open the cell and tear me apart. Instead, she turned and walked away without another word.

"Blind faith is a treacherous path," Clara said as Lila walked by her cell.

"Shut up, you old hag," Lila snarled and shot a bolt of Magic from her fingers at the Soothsayer.

I waited until the outside door *clanked* shut before I spoke. "Are you alright?" I asked Clara.

"I'm perfectly fine. She didn't hit me, and it's not me she's mad at anyway." Shuffling back to her bed and sat down on its edge.

"Do you think I was too hard on her?"

"Maybe, but she needed to hear it. The love she has for her father is one-sided, and the sooner she learns it, the better."

"I never understood how she could love him so blindly when he tossed her around like a dirty dish rag."

"Her father is all she has left in this world. In some way, she suffers from the same sort of loneliness that Violet does," Clara explained.

"Violet?" I asked, furrowing my brow. How could Violet possibly have anything in common with Lila?

"While Lila's heartbreak sits on the surface like an exposed nerve, Violet's runs deep like ocean waters. It gives her strength, but both must be careful not to lose themselves to that loneliness."

"I had no idea." I looked down, ashamed. I knew she struggled with her parent's deaths, especially after Bethany told her the truth, but I hadn't realized how much it still affected her on a daily basis.

"She does a good job of hiding it, but if she is to fulfill her destiny, she will have to face those demons head on." Her brow raised as she leveled her gaze at me. "And she'll need you by her side whether she wants you there or not."

"That's if I ever get out of here," I said, closing my eyes as I let my head fall forward against the bars.

"Tread lightly with Miss Partridge and you might taste freedom sooner than you think," Clara noted.

"You think I got through to her?" My eyes popped open and I eagerly awaited the Soothsayer's response.

Her eyes danced back and forth as she ruminated on my words. "Soon she'll have to choose between her heart and her soul."

"What does that mean?"

"You'll find out soon enough." Clara cooed and turned away from me.

I let out a heavy sigh and moved away from the bars. Soothsayers had their own language sometimes, and it never did any good to dwell on their words.

Sitting down on my mattress, I bit my lip and tried to piece everything together. I started by running down a mental list of the things I did know, beginning with the most pertinent. Aiden wanted Violet dead so she couldn't wake The Lady. Morgana would be brought back from the dead and supposedly there would be no stopping that. But how was she going to come back? And what was with all the ritualistic killings?

Of course we knew why Aiden was searching for the tokens. If he could get to them before we did there would be no way of waking The Lady. He was a smart man to hedge his bets in case Violet did survive the multiple attacks on her life.

I stood and began to pace the small cell. So where did all of this get me? *Ritualistic killings, Morgana, the tokens,* I chanted over and over in my head. As my feet shuffled back and forth on the concrete, I remembered something I'd told Violet: *for every life saved, someone must die.*

My stomach felt hollow and the hairs on the back of my neck stood up. I was onto something. The deaths had to be linked in some way to Morgana, but how?

The outer door slammed closed and I froze mid-thought. Footsteps slowly came down the stairs.

"Ding, ding, ding," Ian's voice echoed down the hall. "Breakfast time." He stopped in front of my cell, holding a tray of food. "I don't normally deliver meals to prisoners, but I thought I'd make an exception for you." He slid the bars open without deactivating the Magical barrier and stepped inside.

I moved across the small space without a word to grab the tray from him.

"Oops," Ian said. He smirked as he let the tray fall to the floor with a loud *clang*. A gooey substance, which I could only assume had been some sort of warm oats, splattered against my shoes and slowly spread across the floor like molasses. A bottle of water bounced once and then rolled over the smooth concrete, coming to a rest as it hit the bars to my right.

"I guess I should have seen that coming," I said with a sigh as I looked at the mess on the floor.

"Tell me what you said to Lila and I'll have one of the guards get you a fresh bowl."

"I don't know what you're talking about," I lied and bent to pick up the water bottle. I knew I had gotten into her head, but I didn't think I'd have confirmation so quickly.

He kicked me square in the stomach and I rolled onto my back, dropping the bottle.

I sucked air through my teeth as pain shot through my body. I was still reeling from the injuries I'd received yesterday, and without the ability to heal myself, I knew the bruising and stiff muscles would only get worse.

"No?" Ian sneered. "Well, that's alright." He kicked me again. "This is much more fun than chitchat." He lifted his leg again. Before he could land another blow, I reached out and grabbed his foot, spun on my knees and elbowed him in the groin.

Ian stumbled backward, holding himself. "Son of a bitch," he cursed.

Pushing myself to my feet, I leaned against the wall for support. "Why don't you just kill me? We both know you want to."

"Believe me, I would like nothing more." Ian panted, sucking down his pain as he stood across the cell from me with a wicked smile pulling at his lips.

An invisible force gripped me by the throat and lifted me off of my feet. Ian walked toward me, his hand raised as if he was holding my neck.

"How can you-" I struggled to get words past the invisible hand crushing my throat.

"How can I use Magic when you can't?" His chest perked up like a bird strutting his feathers, "I'm immune to the tricks of your cage, *Healer*. Now tell me what you said to Lila or so help me, I will snap your neck in two."

I searched his empty eyes as I struggled to breathe. He meant it. He would kill me here and now, regardless of Aiden's wishes. It was time to play nice.

"Alright, I'll tell you," I choked out.

Ian's head twisted to the side as if he was weighing his options. Then he released me.

I coughed, rubbing my neck as I said, "I guess I still have some pull over Lila after all."

"Who do you think you are, playing with her head?" Ian scolded.

"Me?" I said, incredulous. "Aiden is the one lying to her. She thinks he's trying to save the Magical world by stopping Violet from waking The Lady."

Ian smiled and massaged the stubble on his cheeks. "She is easily swayed, isn't she? So desperate to please her father."

My breath started to return and I was able to inspect Ian's expression. "Does that mean you know what Aiden's really up to?" I asked with another light cough.

"Of course." Ian's eyebrows came together on his forehead and he shrugged dismissively. "I'm his trusted number two."

"And Lila? What is she?" I clenched my jaw. I may have despised what she'd done to Violet, but no one deserved to be treated like a pawn by their own family.

"She's a means to an end. If it wasn't for me, he'd have gotten rid of her years ago." He drew his shoulders back and a proud expression adorned his features.

"Wasn't for you..." I balked. How could he honestly think he was some kind of hero?

"I've kept Lila safe. Which is more than you've done for her or Violet," Ian sneered.

Through gritted teeth I said, "Leave Violet out of this."

"Oh did I strike a nerve?" His lower lip protruded in a childish pout as he mocked me.

My hands balled into fists at my side and I fought to keep control of my temper.

"If you cared about her safety, I wouldn't have been able to get anywhere near her when she left the wedding," Ian said with a low chuckle.

"The wedding?" Confusion replaced my anger.

"That's right." He took a step towards me. "You still don't

know." His eyes darkened and a satisfied grin pulled at the corner of his lips. "That was my handiwork you healed."

Without actively telling myself to move, I found my fist flying at his face. He dodged out of the way, but the rage filling my heart propelled me forward. Violet's prone body covered in blood flashed across my eyes. Ian would pay for what he did to her. I swung again, this time connecting with his torso and knocking the air out of him. His shield flew up in front of me just as my knee was about to connect with his nose.

Laughter escaped his throat as he rose to his full height. Fire burned in my chest. I wanted to kill him. As I watched him laugh, I made a promise to myself right then and there that one day I would be the one to end his life.

"You're a sick son of a bitch, you know that?" I cursed, my chest heaving with each breath.

"I've been called worse." He shrugged and kept his shield in place. "As much fun as it's been watching you squirm, I want to know what you told Lila and I want to know now."

"Screw you." I spat at his feet.

He took a step toward me, his hand raised and ready to strike.

"Go ahead, kill me." I stepped toward him. "I'm sure Aiden will be thrilled to hear you disobeyed his orders," I said, taking a huge leap of faith. Ian may have been certifiably crazy, but I hoped he wasn't crazy enough to piss off Aiden.

He hesitated, and I swear if he was an old Saturday morning cartoon smoke would have billowed out of his ears.

A small stunning orb formed in the palm of his hand and before I could move out of the way, it hit me square in the chest. I fell to the ground, my body stiff as it *cracked* against the concrete. I could only watch as Ian stormed out of my cell and everything went black.

———

I woke hours later, my body sore from laying on the cold, hard floor. Late afternoon sunlight drifted through the window high above me and a fresh tray of food had been placed on the bed.

"Finally awake, I see," Clara observed.

"How long was I out?" I rubbed the back of my neck as I stood up.

The old Soothsayer looked up at her own window, making a rough estimate. "About six hours, I'd guess."

I picked up the bottle of water that had rolled away from me earlier and sat down next to the tray on the bed with a heavy sigh.

"I told you not to push that one. He's crazier than a cat trapped in a box."

A short laugh escaped my throat at the image her analogy presented. "I know, but finding out that he was the one who hurt Violet, sent me over the edge," I replied.

"If you plan on getting out of here alive, you can't let your emotions control you." Clara's voice carried a motherly tone as she shook her head with disapproval.

"That's easier said than done." I cracked the seal on the water bottle and took a sip.

"If we are to survive what is to come, you will have to learn to control your emotions and do what is necessary."

I suddenly got the feeling she wasn't just talking about my anger issues with Ian. I moved to the bars and looked toward Clara's cell. She kept her back to me as she leaned against the bars of her own cell.

"Things won't be the same as they were when I get back, will they?" I asked hesitantly.

She turned to look at me. Her gray eyes bore into mine as her lips formed a hard line. "Every day you spend away from

The Waker, the harder it will be when you return," she explained.

I let my forehead rest against the cool bars as her words settled inside me. She was right, of course. Ian and I would have our day, but now was not the time. I needed to focus on getting out of here and getting back to Violet.

"Alright, I'll get myself in check." With my eyes once more locked on hers, I gave Clara a solemn nod.

She smiled and turned away again.

My stomach gave a loud growl as I took another sip of water. I sat back down next to the tray and took a bite of the pasty. The flaky crust made a mess and the contents were lukewarm, but my stomach happily accepted the beef filling.

The pasty wasn't much, but the water helped fill my stomach a bit. I was thankful they chose to feed me. If they were planning to kill me, there'd be no reason to waste food and drink.

Stretching out on my cot, I watched as shadows moved across the walls with the setting sun. As darkness crept in, I thought about my plan to escape and hated that it all hinged on Lila. But if there was another way out of this, I couldn't see it. She was my best chance, and Clara was right. I needed to play my cards right and stop ruffling Ian's feathers. Working him into a blind frenzy wasn't going to help me at all, and I didn't want to give Lila any ammunition to turn on me.

DAY 3

I woke with a feeling of unease in the pit of my stomach. The hair on the back of my neck prickled unnaturally and I dreaded what the day would bring. Sitting up, I brushed the sleep from my eyes and saw Lila standing motionless outside my cage.

I groaned. She had on her wide-eyed innocent look I knew all too well. "Some men might be flattered by the wake up call, but you know how I feel about talking before coffee."

"That's why I brought you this." She wiggled a thermos as she unlocked the gate. "Come on." She coaxed me with a wave of her hand. "Let's go for a walk."

I hesitated, not quite sure what she was up to. Glancing in the direction of Clara, she made one slow, barely perceptible nod. I stood as calmly as I could, the bruises screaming all over my body as my muscles stretched. I felt rigid from head to toe in a way I'd never experienced before. This must have been what it felt like to heal naturally. *How awful,* I thought.

"And where might we be going?" I asked, twisting the lid off the thermos. I sniffed the coffee before taking a hesitant sip.

"I'm not trying to poison you," Lila noted.

A chuckle escaped my throat, "If you wanted to kill me, I'm sure it wouldn't be by poison." Walking through the threshold, I immediately felt my Magic rush to the surface and begin to heal the injuries all over my body. Including a dull headache that had formed behind my eyes while I'd slept. I let out an audible sigh. Not only did I feel like I was in peak physical shape again, but it was an enormous relief to have my Magic back.

"You look better." She looked me up and down and motioned for me to follow her.

"I honestly don't know how people carry on without Magic."

"It's just like anything else." She looked over her shoulder at me. "You don't know what you're missing until it's gone."

"Is that your way of saying you miss me?" I asked, suppressing the urge to kill her right then and there. After everything she'd put Violet through, it was hard to grin and bear it, but I knew she was my best chance of getting out of here.

"Don't flatter yourself." She glared at me sideways and laughed.

As I followed her up the stairs and she opened the door, briny, fresh air brushed against my face. For the first time since we'd arrived, I took a deep breath of the crisp, clean air. The icy breeze chilled my exposed skin and the sky was still dark and gloomy, but I welcomed the change in scenery. It was unseasonably cold for August, which meant we must have been further north of the equator than Pismo. I scanned the area for some indication of where I was, but still found nothing in eyesight that could give me any clue as to where in the world I might be.

"Alright, out with it. You clearly have something on your mind," I said as Lila locked the double doors behind us.

"Not here." She glancing from side to side and started toward the tree line.

I followed after her, curious over what could be so secretive. Maybe I did get into her head and she wasn't completely a lost cause after all. She reached the edge of the tree line before I did and disappeared.

"Lila," I yelled after her, but there was no answer.

My flight instinct kicked in as I stepped over a fallen tree and into the forest. The canopy of leaves above me blocked out most of the sky and I searched all around, ready to make a run for it. I saw no one, Lila had disappeared, and this could be my only chance to escape. The only problem was, I didn't know where I was and had no way of knowing who might help me and who would send me right back to my cell.

Pushing on through the trees, I decided it was best to find out what Lila wanted and put my escape on the back burner until I knew more about where I was. I climbed over large rocks and fallen branches and made my way toward the sound of waves crashing against the shore. I did my best to stay casual, taking another sip of coffee and letting the hot liquid warm me from the inside out.

The trees became thinner the more I walked, and light started breaking through the leaves above. When I reached the edge of the forest, a small beach appeared. My shoes sunk into the sand and made a squishing sound as I moved toward the water. There Lila stood, her golden hair blowing wildly in the wind.

Several small islands sprung out of the water in the distance. They appeared to be uninhabited. Trees and rocks covered every surface I could see. A pang of hopelessness stung my heart, and I knew we were all alone out here.

"So where are we exactly?" I asked, sidling up to Lila.

"Avalon." A small, sad smile pulled at the corner of her mouth.

"Is that right?" I looked out at the water.

Avalon was the mystical island where King Arthur went to recover from the wounds Mordred inflicted on him during his final battle. It was said that once Arthur returned to his full strength, he would return to the throne and command all of England once again.

"At least that's what my father calls it. Officially it's just an island off the coast of Scotland no one cares about."

"Scotland, huh?" If I could get to the mainland, escape would be easy. I had plenty of connections in the UK.

"Yep. It's not my favorite place, but it is undeniably beautiful."

I furrowed my brow, wondering how she was able to orb us here from the Pier as I studied her. In school, Lila had been gifted with spells and potions, but physical Magic was never her strong suit. "When did you learn how to orb?" I asked.

"I didn't." She shrugged and kept her eyes on the stormy gray water. She didn't elaborate. We may have shared everything at one point in time, but now we were both holding our cards close to the chest.

"So, I gather you didn't bring me out here for the view." I shook the thermos from side to side and took another sip.

"I need to know more about The Pieces of Three." She looked at me and I could see the battle waging inside her cerulean eyes. I had to take advantage of this moment and get her on my side without giving her too much information.

"So you believe me then, about Aiden looking for them."

"I didn't say that." She held up her hand, glaring at me defensively.

"What do you want to know?" I turned to face her. My foot sank further into the sand, filling my shoe with a thousand tiny pebbles.

"Why *might* someone be looking for them?" She twisted the ring on her pinky finger and kept her eyes on the ocean.

"You mean, why would Aiden be looking for them?" I corrected her and narrowed my gaze on her profile.

She shifted uncomfortably and crossed her arms.

I sighed, hoping my calm demeanor and sincere concern

would convince her to trust me. "You need The Pieces of Three to wake The Lady. It's the only way." The wind picked up and thunder rumbled overhead as if Mother Nature disapproved of me telling Lila anything about The Lady.

"But I thought Violet was supposed to be the key to waking her. What do The Pieces of Three have anything to do with it?" Lila asked, refusing to remove her eyes from the water.

"Lila, you've got to be straight with me." I touched her arm and she turned to face me. "Did you find something?"

Her eyes met mine and her lips parted. "I think you may have been right about my father searching for them." She looked away, ashamed. "But it doesn't make any sense. He's always said that waking The Lady was the worst thing that could happen to the Magical world, and that's why he wants Violet dead."

"Or maybe he just doesn't want anyone challenging him. Aiden isn't who you think he is," I said with as much sympathy in my voice as I could conjure.

"But if that's true..." she uttered, trailing off as her eyes searched mine for comfort, but I had none to give.

I hardened my face to show exactly how serious things were. "Then that means you tried to kill an innocent woman." I held her gaze. Though part of me wanted to make her pay for what she'd done to Violet, I knew deep down she had no idea what she was doing. Lila was just another victim in Aiden's search for power.

"You don't understand. I had to," she pleaded. "Violet, she's going to bring destruction down on our heads. I didn't have any other choice."

"You always have a choice, Lila," I said. "There was a time when you knew that." I took a step away from her as I watched her world crumble.

"I did what I thought was right - you can't fault me for that." She gazed up at me, the fervent look of realization in her eyes.

"How is killing anyone the right thing to do?"

"You're telling me you wouldn't do what you had to in order to protect your family, your way of life?"

"That's not the point. Violet never did anything wrong, she never hurt anyone. She's been hunted since the day she was born because her destiny is to wake The Lady." A drop of rain landed on the tip of my nose.

"But she'll hurt people," Lila insisted, finding her conviction again. "Including your family." Her voice was cold and hard as the coming rain.

"No, she won't. That's not who she is."

"You always did love blindly." Lila let out a sarcastic laugh.

I didn't dignify her outburst with a response.

"You know, Robert," she said, closing the gap between us. "You think I'm naïve, but the only reason you're defending her is because you let your feelings get in the way."

"That's not true," I replied. Another drop of rain landed on my cheek. The sky was about to open up on us, and I really didn't want to get caught in the storm.

"Isn't it? You can't see anything objectively." She threw her hands into the air in exasperation.

"What I may or may not feel toward Violet doesn't change the fact that you've hurt people. And I don't know about you, but the good guys don't commit murder just because they're told to." I turned around and walked back toward the tree line, pushing through the damp sand.

"Is this really why you brought me out here? To talk about my feelings for Violet?" I called back, pausing to turn around and face her.

She sighed. "No. I just don't know what to do anymore."

"Well, for starters, you need to stop listening to Ian. He's certifiable." I had to yell over the din of the waves and the slow drizzle of rain.

Lila rolled her eyes and said, "He's not so bad."

"Are you kidding me?" I balked, strolling back to her so I

didn't have to shout. "He's one screw loose away from the whole house falling down."

"Don't be dramatic." She rolled her eyes.

"Lila, you need to start thinking for yourself and stop listening to everything daddy dearest tells you." I ran my hand through my damp hair, my patience for decorum running thin.

"You don't understand. He's the only real family I have left."

I thought about what Clara said about Lila being lonely. "You're right, I don't understand. But that doesn't mean you have a free pass." I took a step toward Lila and steeled myself for what had to be done. "You have to know there are other people in this world who care about you," I said, and placed my hand on her shoulder.

"Don't bullshit me, Robert," Lila scolded, swatting my hand away. "You walked away, and never once looked back."

"You're not one of his minions, Lila. You deserve better than that." I wore my emotions on my sleeve, desperately trying to push her in the right direction.

"You're right. I'm not one of his minions, I'm his daughter." She shook her head and crossed her arms. "He wouldn't lie to me."

"Just like he didn't lie to you about your mother?" My eyebrows rose and I took a cautious step closer. This was dangerous territory. The loss of Lila's mother had nearly destroyed her, and I knew this could either go well or horribly bad. But I needed to get her to separate herself from her father.

"He kept the truth from me to protect me," she insisted, glaring at me out of the corner of her eye.

"Is that what he told you?" A sarcastic laugh escaped my throat.

"You think everything is a game don't you?" She turned on me, fists forming at her sides. "I didn't bring you out here so you could play mind games with me."

"Alright." I held up my hands in surrender and took a sip of coffee.

"Now tell me what you know about The Pieces of Three."

Realizing it was time to back off, I answered her question. "Violet needs them in order to wake The Lady. Somehow, she has the ability to activate them and bring The Lady out of her slumber," I explained.

"So if my father can get to them before Violet can, she won't be able to wake The Lady," she said, connecting the dots.

"Right. And I can't let that happen." Thunder roared above us again and the rain picked up, falling at a steady pace and soaking my blood-stained shirt.

"How can you be so sure you're on the right side? We both know The Lady is too powerful for this world. Waking her can only cause destruction."

"And what do you think Morgana will do?" I reached out to her and lightly placed my hand on her arm.

"Morgana is a force to be reckoned with, I'll give you that. But the only thing she's ever wanted is freedom for the Magical world. How can you be against that?" She didn't turn away from my touch this time, but placed her hand on mine. I saw a spark flash across her eyes. She wanted me to understand her side and give her clemency for her sins.

"You're being selective with your history, Lila," I said and let go of her. "Yes, Morgana wanted to be able to practice Magic without the fear of prosecution or exploitation. But she also wanted to gain that freedom by commanding an army whose sole purpose was to destroy all Non-Magical people. Can you really get behind the slaughtering of millions?"

She hesitated a moment and it shocked me. Maybe the girl I was trying to reach was gone. Aiden had really gotten his claws into her this time if she could justify the deaths of an untold number of innocents.

She shrugged and finally said, "No, of course I don't want to see the world's Non-Magical population destroyed. And that's exactly why I went after Violet when my father asked. You're being selective with your history too. The Lady vowed to never help the Magical world again. She swore to destroy us all if we ever woke her. What would you do in my position?"

"Lila, I'm in your position right now. You tried to kill the woman I'm trying to protect. I could easily kill you right here and justify it with your logic." I closed the gap between us and grabbed her arm, pulling her toward me. My emotions were getting the better of me again.

"Go ahead, do it then." She pushed herself against my chest and gave me a defiant glare, her chin jutting out, daring me to harm her.

Magic crackled at my fingertips as Clara's words echoed in my mind. *If you plan on getting out of here alive, you can't let your emotions control you.*

I released her, then turned on my heels and walked back the way we'd come.

"Where do you think you're going?" Lila called after me.

"Back to my cell," I yelled over my shoulder, seething. "I'd rather be locked up without Magic than be out here with you."

How on earth am I supposed to rationalize with a twisted mind like hers? I thought as lightning split the sky in two and a deafening roar crawled across the clouds. The rain started to come down in sheets as I made it under the cover of the trees. Stopping for a moment to take a deep breath, my hands shook with anger. The need to unleash my Magic filled me with anxious energy.

Magic coiled around my hand and I threw a burst of Arcane energy at the nearest tree. Bark exploded around me and a hole the size of a pumpkin sizzled in the center of the trunk.

"You always did have a temper," Lila said, coming up behind me.

"Only when I'm forced to deal with someone who's acting

irrationally," I noted. I kept my eyes straight ahead as we moved through the trees back to my cell without a word.

Hopefully I'd laid enough doubt in her mind because I wasn't sure how much more of this I could take. It was time to start coming up with a Plan B in case this all backfired. I thought I could reach Lila and get her on my side, but the years we'd spent apart had allowed her to form an unhealthy attachment to a psychopath. A small pang of guilt pierced my chest. Maybe if I'd handled things differently, she wouldn't have felt the need to crawl back to Aiden.

As I stepped into the cell, I took one last sip of my coffee and handed the thermos back to Lila. She slammed the bars closed behind her. With the force field back in place, my Magic leeched out of me and I was left feeling defeated.

At this rate, I was never going to get back to Violet.

DAY 7

*D*ays passed since Lila and I spoke on the beach, and neither Ian nor Lila paid me a visit. The only company I had was Clara, who was summoned from her cell a few times, and the guards who delivered my food. Aimlessly, I watched the sunlight move across the floor and fade into darkness each day. I was starting to go mad. My brief and infrequent conversations with Clara were the only things keeping my mind in touch with reality. Maybe I deserved to be locked up and punished for what I'd let happen to Violet. Thinking of her filled my heart with a longing that was almost unbearable. I knew she was safe and alive, but knowing and actually seeing her face, her smile... were two different things. I needed to get out of here.

My prison door slid open with a loud *clang*. Startled, I looked up from where I sat on the bed.

"Aiden wishes to speak with you," Ian said. His voice was stern and he didn't seem too pleased to be fetching me.

"Well Ian, I hate to break it to you but I really don't care what Aiden wishes." I shrugged.

"Get up, *Healer.*" He took a step toward me as if he was about to beat me out of my cage.

I cocked my head to the side and glared at him. "I have a name, you know."

"I said let's go." He closed the distance between us and grabbed me by the arm.

I stood but refused to move forward. I was in no rush to get to Aiden and as an added bonus I enjoyed pushing Ian's buttons. This probably wasn't a good idea, but I'd been light on entertainment for the last couple days and wasn't in the best head-space.

"You think this is a game?" He dropped his hand from my arm and squared himself in front of me.

"Everything's a game and we're all just pawns being moved around a board. Or haven't you learned that yet?" I took a step around him and walked out of my cell.

"Well don't just stand there," I said, looking over my shoulder. My Magic rushed back with a force that almost knocked me off my feet.

His head twitched to the side as he walked past me and unlocked the cell holding Clara. "You too, witch," he demanded.

"Leave her alone." I stepped in front of him and pushed Ian away from the bars.

"I have my orders and so do you. Now move." He shoved me forward and pulled Clara's frail body from her cell.

I was in a testy mood, but I wasn't stupid, so I complied, putting one foot in front of the other up the stairs. The double doors opened and I had to shield my eyes from the blinding light. Ian shoved me forward and a pair of thick-muscled arms caught me. The guard grabbed my wrists and pulled my arms around my back to slap a pair of cuffs on me. My Magic drained out of my body as if I was a battery with a leak.

Damn, that was short-lived, I thought. A guard stood on either side of me, guiding me out onto the lawn. Another guard stood next to Clara and helped her walk toward the house. Odd, they didn't lock her wrists up.

We shuffled through the wet grass up to the estate. The front doors were already open as we walked toward them and every-thing was eerily quiet, no wind, no birds, just silence.

Clara and her guard made their way through the front door first. Just past the foyer, we turned left into a great room. Several people were already in attendance. Lila stood to the right of a large, white marble fireplace and kept her eyes averted as I walked in.

Aiden was sitting in a leather chair adjacent to the fireplace, speaking in hushed tones with a beautiful woman. Her red frizzy curls were at odds with her dark complexion. She was oddly intimidating for someone with such a small frame. She knelt next to him and her eyes searched our faces as we came to a stop at the edge of the Persian rug. She wore a blue power suit that had the same symbol I'd seen on dozens of bodies on the collar of her blazer. Somehow, she was connected to all the ritu-alistic murders, and just like I thought, Aiden must have been behind all of it.

Ian joined Lila where she stood and nodded to the guard holding Clara. The woman speaking with Aiden stood up and Aiden finally cast his sight in our direction.

Clara stepped forward and her guard backed away, moving toward the built-in bookshelf opposite Aiden. She took a slow step forward, and then another. I hadn't realized she was in such a bad physical condition. I could have tried to heal her. Granted, my Magic was being hindered, but all it would take was one touch while I had my Magic and I could help her.

Slowly, she dropped to the dark hardwood floor and sat on her knees in front of Aiden, "You summoned me?" she asked, keeping her eyes on Aiden's black polished shoes.

"The Waker lives," the family patriarch began without

preamble, "but I was told that the spell wouldn't fail. Explain." He laced his fingers together and gave Clara a pointed look.

"It didn't fail." Clara paused as if considering her next words carefully, "It was never completed."

"What do you mean?" Aiden leaned forward, narrowing his eyes.

Lila and Ian shared a concerned look.

"The spell didn't work because it was never completed," Clara repeated.

Aiden shot a glance in my direction.

"She's lying," Lila burst out, and Ian reached for her.

"Forgive me, Lila, but I believe it was you who told me Violet was dead. I'd think twice before you start throwing around the word liar," Aiden warned.

"Father, I'm telling you the truth. I did the spell exactly the same as the rest." She stepped forward, her boots echoing across the hardwood as a few guards blocked her path.

Aiden raised his hand and the guards stepped back into place. "So then what went wrong?" Aiden directed the question to the Soothsayer.

"Like I said, the spell wasn't completed," Clara said.

"Is there something you're not telling me, Soothsayer?" Aiden reached his hand out and lifted her chin so Clara was looking him in the eye.

"Of course not." She held his gaze.

He released her chin and I exhaled. I hadn't realized I'd been holding my breath.

"And what of our other plans?" Aiden inquired as he sat back in the plump armchair and crossed his legs.

"Since Violet survived, you'll still need one more sacrifice, and then she will return to this world," Clara answered.

"The healer will serve as the last sacrifice," Aiden said with a casual wave of his hand.

"Sacrifice? What's she talking about?" Lila looked between Ian and Aiden.

Aiden let out a sigh. "Must you keep interrupting?" He glared at Lila and she recoiled.

"I have the right to know."

"Lila, stop," Ian said under his breath as he tried to restrain her. He gave me a look of pure hatred and I smiled in return.

"You have the right to nothing," Aiden stated. He stood and moved toward Lila, agitation flashing in his uncaring eyes. "You are to follow my orders without question. Are we clear?"

A moment passed where father and daughter stared at each other. A chill ran up my spine as the rest of the room dropped into a tense silence. Ian was the only person who moved a muscle. He reached a hand around the crook of Lila's arm in an attempt to rein her in, but she threw him off.

"I'm your daughter," Lila said, holding her ground and not turning away from her father. "Not one of your minions to be ordered around." She motioned toward the guards in the room.

Aiden chuckled and said, "You may have my blood in your veins, but you're your mother's daughter. Naive and small-minded." He leaned closer to her. "Not one of my minions, you say? Then why have you been running around the world and killing at my request?"

Lila's eyes met mine for a pregnant moment, and I watched as she started shrinking into herself. "I thought we were trying to stop The Lady from being awoken."

Aiden shook his head, laughed and walked back to his seat. "Ian, do you care to tell my daughter what she's really been up to?"

"Sir?" Ian said and stepped forward, his brow furrowed in concern.

"Or better yet..." Aiden sat back down. "Clara, why don't you tell us?" A grin spread across his face. The expression made me feel sick to my stomach.

"One thousand magical souls need to be sacrificed in the name of Morgana in order for her to return from beyond the Veil," the Soothsayer explained.

"Morgana, but you never said anything about her. You said The Lady must not be woken," Lila said, raising her voice as her eyes glassed over with angry tears. She may not have wanted to believe me before, but there was no way she could keep her head in the sand now.

As much as I'd been hoping for this moment, a small part of me wished to spare her the pain of finding out who her father really was. I couldn't imagine how awful I'd feel if I found out my only living relative was a monster.

"The Lady of the Lake is the only one who can defeat Morgana," Clara spoke with solemn care. "If you had succeeded in killing The Waker, then there would be no one to stop her."

"I don't believe you," Lila yelled at Clara and then looked at her father. "You wouldn't, you can't do this!" She stood in front of Aiden as a single tear trailed down her cheek.

"Ian, do you mind," Aiden said with a tired sigh and motioned to have Lila removed.

Ian reached for her arm and she pulled away. "You lied to me all this time." She shoved and elbowed Ian to free herself, but his grip on her shoulders was far too strong. "I've killed for you!" she yelled as Ian dragged her out of the room.

"Maybe you shouldn't follow people so blindly," Aiden suggested as his eyes passed over her like he was bored.

Ian struggled to pull Lila out of the room without knocking over any furniture. As they passed me, her eyes caught mine for a fraction of a second, and then she was gone.

"Thank you for your services once again," Aiden said. He touched Clara's shoulder and she kept her eyes averted from his. "Guard, please escort her back to her chamber." The guard who had assisted her earlier rushed forward and helped her to her feet.

"Bring forward the Healer," Aiden announced. The guards on either side of me moved me forward and forced me down on my knees. "So you're the infamous Robert Maxwell."

I didn't answer, though I refused to look away from him. If it wasn't for the guard's hands on my shoulders, I'd have kicked his teeth in.

"You must be relieved to hear that Violet's alive, are you not?" Aiden goaded me.

I clenched my jaw to fight the insults begging to erupt from my tongue.

"Come now, you must wish to say something."

"Go to hell," I said through gritted teeth. The muscles of my arms strained against my cuffs and the guards had to tighten their hold on me.

"Actually, I prefer to bring hell to us." Aiden smiled and sat back.

"What could you possibly gain from bringing Morgana back into this world?"

"I have everything to gain by returning the rightful monarch to her throne. The Magical World has been running unchecked for far too long. Can you imagine what we could accomplish if we all worked together? This could be our world. We wouldn't have to hide who we really are. That's all Morgana ever wanted," Aiden said. He sat at the edge of his seat with unbridled excitement, and I could see the deranged passion in his eyes.

"Morgana wanted power, not freedom," I corrected, foolishly trying to reason with him.

Aiden smiled. "It's one and the same isn't it?"

"Violet will wake The Lady and stop you."

Aiden shook with laughter and then put his face just inches from mine. "Your precious Soothsayer will join you in death soon enough." He leaned in a little closer to my ear and whispered, "I'm going to enjoy feeling the life drain out of her."

I shot up off of my knees and pushed the guards off of me.

Aiden sat back and put up a shield. I tried to summon my Magic with every fiber of my being, but nothing materialized. The guards were on me again, and one zapped me with just enough electricity to bring me back to the floor.

Aiden laughed and clapped his hands loudly. "Such a show of strength, but we must get down to business. My associate..." he said and looked up at the woman in blue, "has informed me that Violet was without Magic until you healed her, is that correct?"

"Why don't you ask your Soothsayer?" I choked out, fighting the pain rushing through my body.

"She's..." Aiden hesitated. "Limited in her gifts."

"Why would I tell you anything?"

"Do you think you have nothing to lose, Robert? Do you think I can't make your life a living hell until I end it?"

"Go ahead." I held his eyes with mine to show him I wasn't afraid of a little pain.

"If you don't have any care for yourself, what about your family?"

I opened my mouth to insult him further, but hesitated at the mention of my family.

"That's what I thought," Aiden said with a grin. "You wouldn't want them to suffer just because you wouldn't answer a simple question."

I almost shook with anger. "You won't get anywhere near them," I vowed.

"Do you really want to make that bet? I've got someone very close to them right now. All I need to do is give the order."

"You're lying."

"Am I?" His lips pursed together, mocking me.

I kept my mouth shut.

"Fine, how about I demonstrate what's in store for your family," Aiden suggested. He stood and circled behind me, stalking me like prey. "This is going to hurt." I could almost hear the smile in his voice.

He waved his hand over me and fire ripped through me. Every vein in my body felt like lava was coursing through it, but I refused to cry out in pain. I slumped to the floor, unable to hold myself upright as my vision started to blur.

The pain vanished as quickly as it had come. My breathing was ragged and my heart raced like a terrified mouse.

"You're a brave one," Aiden noted as he looked down at me, satisfied. "Now tell me, did she have Magic before you healed her?"

"Screw you," I said and spat at him.

"Very well." He waved his hand again and pain fired through me like a thousand knives. This time it felt like I was freezing from the inside out. I couldn't move, couldn't breathe without icicles stabbing my muscles and bones.

"I can make it stop, just tell me what I want to know," Aiden offered as he hovered over me.

Small noises escaped my throat, but no coherent words came out. Even if I'd wanted to answer him, I couldn't.

Aiden moved back to his chair and waved his hand over me. The ice in my veins vanished and my body temperature quickly rose back to normal.

"I can do much worse, I promise you. So what'll it be?" Aiden asked. He held his hand in a fist and examined his fingernails as I picked myself up off of the floor.

"You think a little pain is going to get me to talk?" I challenged. My voice was ragged and I hardly recognized it.

"Very well then." He raised his hand and all the air was ripped from my lungs. "I'd say you have about sixty seconds before you pass out and maybe two, two-and-a-half minutes before your brain dead."

I gasped for air but couldn't get a breath to save my life. My eyes started to tear up and my lungs burned from a lack of oxygen. I felt dizzy and darkness encroached on my vision.

"Don't think I won't kill you. I can find someone else for the ritual. Maybe your sister, or your brother. Jake, is it?" Aiden asked.

He dropped his hand and a rush of air filled my lungs.

"Last chance to save your family," Aiden promised. "What's it going to be?"

"You really are a monster," I croaked.

"Yes or no?" He fumed. Aiden was clearly past the point of being patient.

"Yes." I coughed as I took another ragged breath. "She was without Magic."

"So it wasn't until after you healed her that she came into her gifts?" The woman in blue asked, standing by the fireplace.

"It would appear that way," I said, looking in her direction.

"Fascinating," she said under her breath. "You're bonded then, correct?"

"I don't know."

"Now, now, Robert. The truth," Aiden cooed.

"I'm telling you the truth. I don't know if we're bonded."

"If they are, it might be worth keeping him alive so I can study him," the slender, dark woman suggested.

"No. If they're bonded, we can't let them have that kind of power. He must die."

"But sir."

"My decision is final, he will serve as the last puzzle piece to release Morgana from her prison beyond the Veil. If you want to run tests, then do it before the week is out." Aiden stood and adjusted the cuff of his shirt. "Take him back to his chamber and let the guards know that Alyssa may have full access to him," he said to the two men still holding onto me and left the room.

"I'll be visiting you shortly, Mr. Maxwell," Alyssa said, giving me an eager smile before following Aiden.

The guards allowed me to stand and we walked back to my prison in silence.

I wished I knew what was going on with Lila. She'd made

such a scene, and it was clear that she had been manipulated into doing her father's bidding. It would have been better for us both if she hadn't gone toe-to-toe with Aiden in front of everyone, but there wasn't much I could do about that now. I had to admit, I was relieved she finally knew the truth about Aiden, but now the entire compound would be watching her like a hawk and escaping would be that much harder.

DAY 8

nother sunrise and another sunset, and still I was no closer to getting home. Laying on my lumpy mattress in my blood-stained shirt and dusty jeans with my arm over my eyes, I tried to imagine I was lying on Violet's couch. Clara paced in her cell and I let myself believe it was Violet, padding around the kitchen. My memory kicked up the image of her in tiny cotton shorts and a baggy Beatles t-shirt making coffee. My chest swelled and more than ever I wished I could see her face again, hear her voice.

Tap, tap, tap. The sound of metal clinking against metal made me sit up straight.

"Hello, Robert. May I join you?" Alyssa asked, standing outside my cell. Her ringed finger was still touching one of the bars.

"Like I have a choice," I mumbled, annoyed that she had interrupted my brief reverie.

"I'm not here to hurt you. I would just like to gather some information."

"Whatever you say," I sighed as she stepped inside.

She put her silver case on the bed next to me, popped the

latches and pulled out a pair of black gloves along with a small leather pouch.

"I'm going to take some blood from you," she said, unrolling the black pouch and producing a needle and a few empty vials.

"What do you want my blood for?" I asked.

"I have an interest in genetics, and I'd like to see if there is anything in particular that allows you to pass on Magic through your ability."

"Other Healers aren't able to do the same?" She piqued my interest. I had often wondered why I was able to pass my Magic to Violet.

"None that I've worked with." She shrugged. "There's something unique about you and Violet. I'm hoping to find the anomaly that allowed you to transfer Magic, so I can reproduce it."

I looked Alyssa over once more and hesitated. The last time someone experimented with Magic, Chernobyl went nuclear and killed a couple dozen people. But what other choice did I have? If I refused, the guards outside my cell would storm in and force the blood out of me. Reluctantly, I nodded my consent. She knelt down in front of the bed and took my forearm in her hand. Wrapping a tourniquet around my bicep, she began to feel for the veins in the crook of my arm. I watched her with curious eyes. Her coarse, red hair sprang out in tight curls all over her head, and her complexion was more than just sun-kissed. Her features were different from anyone I'd ever met, and I wondered what her genetic makeup might be.

"I know that look," she said with a smile.

"What do you mean?" I studied her smooth features. She wasn't like anyone else I'd met here. There was a calm confidence about her that made me wonder how she fit in with Aiden's group.

"My appearance is unique. People are always curious."

"I didn't mean to be rude."

"Not at all." She dismissed my words with a quick wave of her manicured hand. "I'm half Scottish, half Ethiopian."

"That's an interesting mix," I noted.

"Make your hand into a fist for me." She tapped the veins on my arm. "There we go." Pushing the needle into my arm, she connected the first empty vile.

"My parents were very interesting people," the woman explained. "My mother's family immigrated to the UK when she was just a girl. She ended up working for Aiden's father as a guard at one of his labs. That's how she met my father. They hit it off right away, but my dad wasn't Magical so they had to hide their affair. It wasn't until my mother got pregnant that they finally came forward. Luckily, my father was able to convince Mr. Partridge senior that my mother should have me so they could study me once I was born. They didn't know much about human and Magical births back then and I was the perfect subject."

"So they experimented on you?" I asked. I did nothing to hide the horrified look on my face.

"They took blood samples every few weeks and charted my development, but they never hurt me. My father made sure of that."

"Why are you telling me this?" I shook my head and adjusted myself on the bed, making the springs *squeak* in protest.

"So you'll see that not all of us are monsters." She looked up at me, wide-eyed and innocent. I wasn't buying it. She may play the sweet and wholesome act, but she couldn't have ended up in Aiden's company without having a few sharp edges.

"Experimenting on your own children sounds pretty horrific to me," I noted.

"Without science, we wouldn't know as much as we do about Magic. Studying how each gift works gives us a better understanding of what the limitations are."

"And let me guess, Aiden wants to know how I was able to pass on my Magic to Violet so he can recreate the effect?"

"You don't miss a thing." Alyssa looked up at me from under her eyelashes.

"And you're okay with helping that psychopath?"

"I'm not helping him, he's helping me. Without his support and resources, I wouldn't have access to people like you," she pointed out as she switched the full vile for an empty one.

"People like me? You mean prisoners." I scoffed at how casual she was about the fact that I was here against my will.

She sighed and said, "He's not as bad as you make him out to be."

"Please tell me you're joking." My eyes almost fell out of my head. How could everyone around here be so naïve? Could Aiden really be that charismatic?

"He wants to help the Magical world and give you freedom."

"And you think Morgana is the way to do that?"

"Morgana was mistreated in her time. All she ever wanted was to be recognized for who she really was. That's something all Magical people can relate to, right?"

"Being recognized for your gifts and wanting to rule the Magical world are two completely different things."

"Well then, we'll have to agree to disagree." She switched the full vile of blood with the last empty one.

We sat in silence while my blood trickled into the clear tube hanging from my arm. She pulled the needle out once she had everything she needed, leaving a tiny drop of blood on my skin.

"Can you release the Magical barrier so he can heal himself?" Alyssa asked.

One of the guards waved his hand over the lock on my cell and the blue force field shimmered, then fell away.

"Thanks." The tiny pinprick in my arm disappeared and my Magic returned.

"If I may." She reached for my arm again.

I held my forearm out and she wiped away the blood, looking at the smooth skin where she had just pricked me.

"Incredible," she said with a smile. "This next bit is a little messier." She rolled up the sleeve of her blazer, pulled a scalpel from her bag and cut a deep wound in her forearm.

"What the hell are you doing?" I exclaimed and shot to my feet.

"Heal me." Her face remained emotionless and her voice was steady as she extended her arm toward me. Dark drops of blood splattered onto the dusty gray floor as I stared at her, horrified.

"Go on," she encouraged as she pushed her outstretched arm toward me.

I exhaled loudly as I grabbed her wrist and released my Magic. I could feel the warmth spread through my arm to hers and heal each layer of tissue and flesh. The wound stitched back together on a cellular level, healing not just the tear in her skin, but rebuilding the nerves and fibers that made up her arm. With little effort on my part, the bleeding stopped and the wound closed up nicely.

"Please don't do that again," I said, releasing her.

She removed a towel from her bag and wiped the blood from her wrist.

"Not even a scar." She turned her arm from side to side.

"You've had your fun, now I think it's time for you to go," I said, turning away from her. Was everyone here certifiably crazy? Who willingly harms themselves like that?

"Here, clean yourself up." She threw a clean towel toward me. "There are a few more details I'd like to go over before I leave you." Her high heels *clicked* across the floor as she moved to the bed and pulled out an odd-looking, clear box from her bag. The box had a slit in the middle big enough to fit a hard-back novel. Moving her case, she sat down on the bed with the contraption in her lap and tapped the empty place next to her.

I moved toward her but wasn't in the mood to sit. "What is that?" I asked, nodding at the box.

She picked it up and said, "This will take measurements as you use your healing ability." She pressed something on the clear surface and it sprang to life. A menu appeared across the top and she pressed a few buttons on the touchscreen.

I had never seen anything like it before and had no idea you could even measure Magic. A warning bell went off in the back of my mind and I knew I should stay far away from Alyssa.

"Please, take a seat so we can proceed."

"I've had enough of this," I said, backing away from her.

"Robert, I would rather you did this willingly, but I will use force if I have to." She eyed me and the mask of calm curiosity she wore faded. She sat, shoulders back, completely upright with a flat expression in her eyes that left me with no doubt that she would bend me to her will, one way or another.

I steeled myself for whatever experiment she had planned next and sat next to her.

"Now, this will hurt a bit," she said as she pulled a scalpel out of her bag of tricks. "Your palm, please." She held her hand out for mine.

The list of people I wanted to do physical damage to was growing day by day. I put my hand in hers, palm up, and she drew the scalpel from my wrist to my fingers.

"Don't heal yourself just yet," she said as she etched another gash into my hand.

Blood covered my palm and dripped onto the bed. I cringed at the pain but kept my hand steady. She placed my hand in the box and touched a few options on the screen.

"Okay, now," she urged, her bright blue eyes alight with excitement once again.

I released my Magic and my hand stitched itself back together. My heart rate appeared on the top right corner of the screen. Graphs and other readings appeared all over the top of the apparatus in different colors as the gash in my hand disappeared.

Alyssa's eyes widened in excitement as the device came to life. "Fascinating."

Pulling my hand out of the contraption, I wiped the blood off with the towel she had given me.

"That was excellent. Thank you, Robert," Alyssa said with a satisfied smile.

"What did that do exactly?" I rubbed my palm.

"It takes your vitals, measures the Magical output, and just gets a basic reading on everything that's happening while you use your ability."

"I've never seen anything like that before." I stood up and moved across the cell. Just sitting next to her was making me anxious.

"You wouldn't have. It's my own creation." She beamed. "Have you had enough time to heal?" She examined me curiously.

"I'm fine." I folded my hands behind my back.

"Good. You can put the Magical barrier back up," she said over her shoulder to the guard. "Sit, Robert, please. I just want to ask you a few questions." She pulled a tablet from her bag and placed it on her lap.

"I'll stand, thank you," I replied.

"So be it. You said that Violet didn't have Magic before you healed her. Are you certain of that fact?"

"Yes." I folded my arms across my chest as she made notes on the tablet.

"And have you healed anyone before?" She crossed one leg over the other.

"Yes, but just minor injuries, nothing fatal..." Looking up at the small window above my head, I thought back to the few times I'd healed friends and family. I tried not to abuse my ability, but a handful of times I just couldn't stand to see my loved ones in pain when I could do something about it.

"Did you and Violet know each other before she was injured?"

"You mean before Aiden sent someone to kill her? No, we didn't know each other." An image of Violet standing in the bookstore, looking up at me flashed across my eyes.

"You're sure?" Alyssa pressed on and narrowed her gaze like she could see what I was thinking.

"I'm sure, dammit."

"In your opinion, was Violet dying when you healed her?"

"That's enough, I'm done." I walked to the other side of the cell. I wanted to slam a door, shut her out, but as I was trapped behind bars, I settled for leaning against the back wall with my arms crossed.

"I know this isn't easy, Robert, but I need you to answer the question," Alyssa urged, ignoring my obvious signs of protest.

"I'm not your lab rat," I snapped and took a step toward her.

She blinked, unmoved by my anger, which only made me more furious.

"You come in here and tell me all about your family history to get me to... what, feel sorry for you?" I blurted out. "Well guess what, I don't. You may say you're not a monster, but you sit there and passively talk about life and death like it's some sort of toy for you to play with."

"I know your pain, Robert." She stood and stepped toward me, her heels echoing like a judge's gavel handing out a sentence. "I used to feel the same way as you. But science, it saved my mother's life. With science, we can study the unknown and help people cheat death. Your gift could hold the key to saving millions of lives. Don't you want to be a part of that?" She placed her hand on my arm and her eyes pleaded for me to understand.

"You can't cheat death," I said through gritted teeth and removed her hand from my arm.

"But we can, by studying gifts like yours."

"Death is a part of life. You can't change that without dire consequences."

"When you experiment as I do, there are always consequences," she said flippantly. "But it's all for the greater good. Can't you see that? The more we can learn about your ability and how you were able to pass your Magic to Violet, the more good we can do in the world."

"You may want to help people, but we both know Aiden has entirely different plans for the knowledge you acquire." I narrowed my eyes and held her gaze.

"What Aiden chooses to do with the information I give him is out of my control." She looked away from me and turned on her heel. "Just know that everything I do, I do for the greater good."

"Yeah, well something tells me we don't see eye to eye on what the greater good is."

"Maybe not. But that doesn't mean I'm your enemy."

I didn't buy one line of her whole innocent act. Working with Aiden, even if she didn't agree with everything he did, made her my enemy. Granted, she wasn't first on my list, but she would still need to be dealt with at some point. I knew first hand, experimenting with Magic never ended well.

"Are we done here?" I asked as she started putting everything back in her case.

"For now," she said with a smile and flipped the lock on her kit. "It really is a shame that Aiden wants to sacrifice you for the ritual." She closed the gap between us. "There is much we could learn from someone with your gift," she whispered. At the close proximity of our bodies, I could smell the sickly sweet perfume she wore and it turned my stomach.

Alyssa stepped away from me and the guards slid the cell

open for her. "Until we meet again, Mr. Maxwell," she said over her shoulder. "Oh, and do give my best to your cellmate?"

"Clara?" I asked and stepped closer to the bars.

She nodded. "Her cooperation in helping us understand her gift has been very useful already. You may want to take a page out of her book."

"Not likely." I met her eyes and Alyssa smiled before moving along.

Her high heels *clicked-clacked*, each step echoing as she walked down the concrete path and up the stairs. I let out a sigh of relief when I heard the door close behind her. Jumping across my cell in one stride, I checked to see if Clara was back yet. They had taken her early this morning and her cell remained empty. I hadn't realized how lonely I was without her presence. Even if we weren't talking, it was just nice knowing someone else was there with me. I wondered where she could be and hoped they weren't hurting her.

DAY 9

*M*y body shook back and forth and distantly, I heard someone whisper, "Robert, wake up."

I rolled onto my side and blinked through bleary eyes to see Lila hovering above me. A jolt of panic ran through me and in an instant I was on my feet. "What, what is it. What's wrong?"

"We have to go," she said and looked over her shoulder, "now."

"We?" I asked and rubbed the sleep from my eyes.

"I promise I'll explain later, but we need to go now." She held her hand out to me.

The panicked look in her expression propelled me forward. "Lead the way."

We made our way past the empty cages. Clara stirred as we came near.

"Wait, we can't leave her behind," I said as loud as I dared.

"Robert, we don't have time. They're coming for you, for the ritual. We have to go now," she whispered with harsh impatience.

"Go, my place is here," Clara said as she stood and shuffled across her cell.

"But-" My fingers gripped the bars of her cell.

"It's alright. Get back to Violet." Clara gave my hand a firm squeeze. "And be careful with her." Her eyes shot in Lila's direction.

"Robert," Lila hissed.

I nodded and Clara backed away from the bars into the shadows.

Lila and I went up the stairs, through the double doors, and across the manicured grass to the tree line at a brisk jog. The cool, early morning air caressed my skin, leaving a trail of goosebumps. The sky was pitch black and the only light came from the full moon overhead. Neither one of us spoke, and I kept my guard up as we hiked up a hill through the cover of the trees. *This could be a trap, I thought. Lila could be leading me to my death.* But something inside me trusted her. We'd known each other for years, and even though we'd both changed, I could see the terror in her eyes when she woke me. Lila wanted off this island as badly as I did.

"We're almost there," she huffed, out of breath.

"And where is that exactly?"

"We're getting the hell out of here."

I stopped abruptly. "We can't just leave, we have to try to stop the ritual." I started to turn back.

"Robert, wait," Lila said, running after me and pulling on my arm. "If you go back, he'll kill you." Her eyes glistened in the moonlight.

"I can't just stand by and let Aiden bring Morgana back from the dead." I pulled my arm from her grasp. "She's the worst thing that could ever happen to the Magical World."

Lila sighed and shook her head with resignation. "Fine, but let's do this quickly then." She began jogging through the trees back the way we'd come.

We backtracked about fifty yards, and then Lila took an abrupt left turn over a large grouping of rocks.

"Are you sure you know where you're going?" I asked as we started to go uphill again.

She gave me a pointed look over her shoulder and smiled. "I forgot how much you hate not being in control."

"I was just making-" The night sky lit up red like a flash from a camera, cutting me off. We both stopped in our tracks and our eyes caught.

"Looks like he found someone else to sacrifice for the ritual. That means he knows you escaped, and he'll assume I helped since I'm not down there." Lila stumbled back a few steps. "Now we really need to leave."

"I'm not going anywhere until I stop him." I moved in the direction the flash of light had come from.

"It's already too late." Lila stepped in front of me and placed her hand on my chest.

"You can either help me or get out of my way," I said, tossing her hand off of me.

"Fine then." She pushed past me. "But so help me God, Robert, if I die tonight I'll haunt you for the rest of your miserable life." She turned away from me and ran through the trees.

It was clear she knew this island intimately. Her feet glided effortlessly through the brush, jumping over stumps and climbing over large rocks like she'd been doing it her whole life. As I followed behind her, I couldn't help but be impressed by her strength. Lila had risked her life and forsaken her family to save me, and now here she was leading me right back to them. As much as it pained me to think it, I was glad to see the woman I knew years ago was still in there somewhere.

Clara's words echoed in my head, *"She must choose between her heart and her soul."*

Lila soon slowed to a walk. "We're almost there," she whispered and pointed towards the blue light coming through the trees.

As we quietly made our way to the tree line, the dull blue

glow became blinding. I shielded my eyes as we came to the edge of a cliff. Twenty-five feet below us, in a large empty field, Aiden and a few of his followers stood in a semi-circle in front of what looked like a portal. I crouched down to get a better look, stunned that Aiden was able to conjure up a portal at all. I had heard about them in legends, but no one in a thousand years had actually seen one.

"See, I told you it's already too late." The blue glow illuminated her face with an unnatural light as she spoke, making her look pale. Her eyes stayed fixed on the sight below as she placed her hand on my arm.

"It isn't too late until Morgana walks through that portal," I said and threw my legs over the side of the cliff, searching for a foothold.

"What the hell are you doing?" Lila shot forward on her hands and knees, grabbing my forearms.

"I'm going down there. I have to try something, anything, to stop him."

"Robert, look, I get it, you're the good guy. But if you go down there, the only thing you'll accomplish is an untimely death."

"Lila-"

"No," she cut me off. "What does the prophecy say?"

"What?"

"Tell me, what does the Prophecy say about Morgana?" She held me still with a fierce glare.

"That she can only be defeated by The Lady of the Lake."

"And Violet is the key to waking her, right?"

"Yes, but-" I dug my foot into the side of the cliff.

"No buts, let's get out of here while we still can."

The ground began to shake and thunder rolled across the cloudless sky. I nodded and started to pull myself up.

"We'll need to hurry. I need a direct eye line to the full moon if I'm going to pull this off," Lila urged.

Lightning crackled and exploded above us as hurricane-force winds blew all around us, throwing leaves and dirt into the air. My fingers slid through the dirt as I lost my footing.

"She's coming through," I yelled over the noise as I tried to pull myself back over the edge. But the wind was too strong and I struggled to hold on. Just as my fingers lost their grip, Lila reached out and grabbed my wrists. Summoning her shield behind her, she was able to block out most of the wind and help pull me back over the edge.

I collapsed on top of her and her shield vanished. Branches, leaves, and rocks flew toward us at dangerous speeds. Grabbing Lila's hand, I crawled over to one of the large trees. We both wrapped our arms around the trunk for support and put up our shields to protect us from flying objects.

"Just hold on a little longer. It should pass once Morgana enters our world," I yelled to Lila.

She nodded and squeezed my hand tighter. A large branch came flying at us and ricochet off our shields like a Frisbee. The hammering of rocks and leaves hitting my shield was deafening. I felt like my eardrums would explode at any moment, and then the wind stopped. Everything fell to the earth with a loud crash and the air became still. I looked over at Lila and we both let our shields slip away. Without a word, we edged closer to the cliff, both of us needing the confirmation that Morgana had really been brought back from the dead.

A naked woman, her skin pale as ivory and her hair as black as ink, emerged from the luminescent blue portal. One of Aiden's men ran forward, dropped to his knees in front of her and presented her with a dark, silk robe.

She reached out gingerly, keeping her eyes on the men in front of her as she plucked the robe from the gentleman's outstretched arms. The portal behind her began to fizzle and burn out as she took her first step toward Aiden. In one swift motion, she wrapped the robe around her slender figure and pulled it tight as she took another step.

Watching her was intoxicating. She moved with such grace and power it was no wonder men fell at her feet to serve her.

"Time to go," Lila whispered in my ear as Morgana's eyes shot up and landed on us still hidden in the trees. She couldn't possibly see us, could she?

Morgana raised her arm and one delicate finger pointed directly at us.

"Shit," we said in unison as everyone's heads turned in our direction.

Scrambling through the foliage, we made a run for it with Lila leading the way. Everything looked completely different as we headed back the way we'd come. Trees had been uprooted, leaving behind gaping holes we had to dodge as we ran in the dark. Only the faintest glimmer of moonlight broke through the canopy above us.

When we reached a wall of rocks, I glanced over my shoulder. A yellow glow was bouncing through the trees behind us. Someone was coming.

"We'd better hurry," I said, nudging Lila ahead and giving her a boost.

Pulling myself onto the first small landing, I began to climb over each boulder, careful to make sure my feet were steady before I reached for the next rock. Lila made it to the top in no time and started down the other side. Once I reached the top, I waved my hand over the rocks and uttered, *"Levis."* The grooves and edges of the rocks reformed and became smooth as a slide. No one would be able to follow us this way now. They would have to go around and that would buy us at least a few minutes.

Jumping down as the rocks finished reforming under my feet, I hit the ground and rolled to keep my momentum. Lila was already running up the hill about fifteen feet ahead of me. I followed behind and quickly closed the gap. It was clear she was getting off this island with or without me, so I needed to stick close.

The trees began to thin out the further we ran, and the moon was now visible above us.

"We almost there?" I called out to her.

"Just about." Lila slowed to a jog. "We just need to get to the top, right there." She pointed to about twenty feet ahead of us.

Catching up to her, I turned to see if anyone was close behind us. The trees were dark and quiet where I scanned them.

Lila pulled a vile out of her bag as she reached the top of the hill. Stepping out into the moonlight, she bent down, picked up a handful of dirt and began to recite a spell I'd never heard before.

"*Aufer a me huc, invenio tutum locum,*" she recited.

Lila raised the vile toward the moon, and the opaque liquid began to glow. She closed her eyes and swallowed the contents in one swift motion.

"Come on, we're getting out of here," she said, reaching her hand out to me.

I heard a branch snap just as I saw the shadow come into view. "You're not going anywhere," Ian said and stood a few feet below us. He held a crude sort of weapon and looked disheveled, making him appear as deranged as he actually was.

"I'm going to enjoy this," I said under my breath as I made a run at him. I knew better than to make the first attack, but my hatred for him propelled me forward. Taking one last step, I summoned a freezing spell. Blue sparks shot from my fingertips as I slid and kicked his feet out from under him.

Jumping back onto my feet, I readied myself for him to strike back. "I told you, you weren't her type," I said. I couldn't help but grin as he tried to get up. I threw another freezing spell at his chest and he crumpled into the leaves and rolled a few feet down the hill.

"Robert, let's go!" Lila yelled.

I took another step toward Ian.

"We have to go now!" Lila shouted, her voice urgent.

I turned away from Ian and ran back up to Lila.

"Grab my hand." she reached for me.

"I thought you didn't know how to orb?"

"I don't, just trust me." She motioned for me to grab her hand again. "You've got to be kidding," she exclaimed as her gaze landed somewhere behind my shoulder.

Lila's face started to glow as if she was carrying a candle. I looked back toward Ian just in time to see a fireball coming right at us. She threw herself at me and we tumbled to the ground, narrowly avoiding the ball of fire that exploded where my head had just been.

We quickly stood and faced Ian as he charged toward us.

"That's enough, Ian!" Lila yelled, and at the wave of her hand he went flying and smacked into a tree.

"You can't do this, Lila. You're one of us," Ian growled from all fours as he tried to catch his breath.

"Not anymore," she said with so much venom Ian physically flinched at her words.

"You know what this means, don't you?" Ian stood up and brushed the dirt from his clothes.

"That you'll have to kill me." Lila grabbed my hand. "I'd like to see you try." She whispered something under her breath and everything swirled around us. My feet dangled below me, searching for solid ground, and we fell aimlessly through a tunnel of debris.

When the howling of the wind slowed, the outline of a building came into view and we landed roughly in a patch of grass. I lay still for a moment to catch my breath and stared up at the stars.

"We should be safe for now, but they'll be able to track us. We're going to have to go the rest of the way without Magic," Lila explained.

I stood up and looked around. Floodlights lit up the ruins of a castle and the moon reflected off a large body of water in front of us. "Quick question. Where in the hell did you transport us?"

A nervous laugh escaped her throat. "I was in a rush and didn't have time to work out our coordinates beforehand, but I believe were in the UK."

"Wonderful. We're lost and we can't use Magic."

Lila waved off my irritation. "People get lost without Magic all the time, we'll be fine."

I looked around for some sign of where we were. If floodlights were directed onto the castle ruins, that meant it was probably a tourist attraction. Up the hill above us, I saw a railing with plaques spread about twenty feet apart.

"Bingo," I said, and started trudging up the steep hill.

"Where are you going?" Lila called after me, but I ignored her.

As I climbed over the railing, Lila appeared next to me. "You could have just taken the stairs," she said and pointed to the left where concrete stairs led up to the lookout.

I gave Lila a disparaging look and hoofed it to the closest sign. It was a drawing of the ruins below and was labeled *Urquhart Castle.*

"Do you have a phone on you?"

Lila dug through her bag and handed me her phone.

I opened the Maps icon typed in *Urquhart Castle.* "You've landed us on top of Loch Ness."

"At least we're not far from Inverness," Lila said with a smile.

I shook my head, cracked the phone in half and tossed it in the nearest bin.

"Looks like we've got a long walk ahead of us," I said with a sigh and made my way past the visitor center up to the main road.

"*M*orning, sunshine," Lila's chipper voice pierced my ears.

"I forgot you're a morning person," I said as I slowly crawled out of bed.

"There's coffee on the nightstand." A nondescript paper cup sat next to the hotel lamp.

"Where did this come from?"

"Downstairs. I thought about venturing out, but we don't know who might be following us."

"Thanks," I said, tipping the cup in her direction and taking a sip. I sighed in relief, desperately thankful for the warmth and comfort of a cup of coffee after the night we'd had. Inverness was one of those towns that shut down early. We had walked for several hours before we were able to flag down a car to take us the rest of the way.

Stretching my arms above my head, I cracked my back. It had been awhile since I'd slept in a comfortable bed. Not that I minded sleeping on Violet's couch with her in the next room. The thought of her sent a jolt through me and my Magic hummed anxiously. I wished we were still linked by the connection spell so I could get a glimmer of her emotions. I thought maybe once we were off of Avalon I might be able to feel something, but I couldn't even get the faintest echo of her.

"Since we're partners in crime now, do you mind telling me what happened to the connection spell I had on Violet?" I asked.

"You know, I don't know. We never took it off you," she said while running a brush through her golden hair. "They must have removed it on her end."

I pursed my lips, frustrated. "I need to get in touch with my family." I stood and walked toward the restroom.

"I don't think we should contact anyone, not until we're back in the States," Lila advised, twisting a ring on her pinky finger. It was a nervous tick of hers and made me wonder if there was something she wasn't telling me.

"What is it?" I reached out and stopped her fiddling.

She looked away from me toward the window. "I saw Ian this morning."

"You met with him?" My eyebrows shot up and the muscles in my shoulders tensed.

"No, of course not." She rolled her eyes. "I saw him through the window while I was downstairs getting us coffee." She quickly glanced up at me and then away. "They know we're here, in Inverness."

"Alright, then it's time to leave. I don't suppose you have any more of that orbing potion?" I asked, hopeful. If she did, it would make getting back to Pismo so much easier.

"I used the last of it to get us off, Avalon." Her eyes shifted from side to side.

I sighed. I knew getting home wouldn't be easy, but one break would be nice. "I have a contact in London who may be able to help us. But first things first. We need to get the hell out of dodge before they find us."

"Okay," she said as she moved across the room and picked up the few items she had unpacked.

"How much cash do you have on you?" I asked as I stepped into the bathroom to rinse my face.

"After we pay for the hotel, about five hundred pounds. I wasn't able to grab much."

"That's plenty for now. We'll need to get to the train station and get out of here as soon as we can." I turned the faucet on and splashed some cold water on my face.

"Where are we headed?"

"Not sure yet, but definitely south." I threw another handful of water on my face and scratched the stubble along my jaw.

"I left some clean clothes for you in the bathroom," Lila said nonchalantly as she picked up the bulky hotel phone. "I'll call downstairs and see if they have a train schedule."

Kicking the bathroom door closed, I noticed the clean button-up and jeans sitting on the counter. I barely recognized myself when I looked at my reflection in the mirror. My hair stood out in unnatural directions, and the beard I'd grown over the last week and a half hid the shape of my jaw. Stripping my clothes off, I jumped in the shower. The warm water felt good on my muscles. My Magic may have healed all my injuries, but the memory of the pain had stayed with me. I let the water wash over me and remove the dirt and blood caked onto my skin.

My mind drifted to Pismo as I scrubbed a dollop of shampoo into my hair. How was I going to explain Lila to my family, to Violet? A knot formed in the pit of my stomach as I imagined the look of betrayal in Violet's eyes. I needed Lila to escape, that much I could explain; but why she was still with me, no one would understand. We may have escaped Aiden, but our battle was far from over.

Reluctantly, I turned the water off and finished getting ready. The shirt and jeans Lila had grabbed for me fit perfectly. She had always been good at remembering the little things. Feeling as much like myself as I possibly could, I walked back into the bedroom and found Lila sitting on the bed, sniffling.

I cleared my throat and asked, "You alright?"

"Fine." She wiped her face with both hands but couldn't hide her red nose or glassy eyes. "We're all set," she continued and popped up from the bed. "A taxi is coming to get us in about ten minutes to take us to the station. I booked us on a train to Perth. I figured that was far enough away from here and still central enough so we can get another train going wherever we need."

"Perfect. Let me make a quick phone call and then we'll be on our way." I crossed the room and picked up the receiver off the nightstand and swiftly dialed the number I had memorized years ago.

After three rings, a woman's voice came through the receiver, "This is Katherine, how may I be of service?" The familiar voice was a warm welcome.

"Hi Katherine, Robert calling for Malcolm."

Malcolm, a trusted friend and Promised One has gotten me out of plenty of tight situations over the years. He's the one and only person I could trust to help us now.

"How's your wife?" she asked, using the secret phrase Malcolm and I had agreed upon many years ago.

"Three sheets to the wind," I replied. The line went quiet and I was transferred.

"Robert, it's been awhile, I was starting to think you'd finally gone straight and didn't have a need for me anymore," Malcolm said with his typical good humor.

I laughed. "That'll be the day."

"So what can I do for you?" His husky voice came through the receiver and I pictured him leaning back in his chair with his feet on his desk.

"I need to get state-side undetected."

"Sure, sure not a problem. When do you need to get out?" he asked without skipping a beat.

"As soon as possible. But there's something else. I have someone with me. She'll need documents as well."

Malcolm's hearty smoker's laugh bellowed through the receiver. "I'm going to need to hear this story one day, my friend."

I rolled my eyes. "Yeah, yeah. It's not what you think."

"It never is with you. What's the girl's name so I can get her paperwork set up?"

"Well, err...It's Lila."

"You're with Lila again, are ya?"

I sighed at the grin behind his voice and said, "Like I said, it's not what you think."

"Whatever you say," he chuckled. "Where are you coming from this time?"

"Inverness. We're leaving shortly, though, headed to Perth. It's getting a little cramped here for my taste."

"Right, say no more. Do you remember the drop location in Glasgow?"

"Glasgow Central," I confirmed.

"One week," he said.

"Thanks, Mal. I owe you one."

I hung up the phone and when I stood up from the bed Lila was leaning against the door with her arms folded across her chest and a scowl on her face.

"Was that Malcolm Ward?" she asked, keeping her eyes on the ground.

"Yes, is that a problem?" I replied, eyeing her.

"You know he hates me, right?"

"Can't say I blame him." I shrugged.

Her head shot up as she pushed off the wall and began to pace around the room. "Thanks."

"Relax," I said, gathering my very few belongings. "He's nothing but professional."

"Are you sure?" She paused and bit her lip.

"Positive." I maneuvered around her, picking up my shoes and sitting down to put them on.

"So we're headed to Glasgow then?"

"We are, indeed," I replied, slipping my shoe on. "We'll stay in Perth until it's time to move on to Glasgow. It'll take Malcolm a week to get everything together, but he'll be able to supply us with passports and tickets back to the states."

"A week?" Lila exclaimed.

"If you want to get out of here safely then yes, a week."

She let out a heavy sigh. "I was hoping to get out of here as quickly as possible."

"A week is as quick as it's going to get."

"Okay, just..." her voice was hesitant.

"What is it?"

"Just promise me you won't leave me behind." She bit her lip and kept her eyes averted. "My father won't hesitate to kill me if they find me."

"Lila, you have a lot to make up for. But after everything that happened on Avalon, I believe you had no idea what Aiden was really up to." I stood beside her and put my hand on her shoulder. "I promise I won't leave you behind."

She nodded and cleared her throat before saying, "Thank you." The worry lines in her face vanished as we made our way downstairs.

I wasn't sure how I was going to explain why I'd returned with Lila, but I couldn't just leave her. Aiden would surely kill her for her betrayal, and as much as I still despised her for what she'd done to Violet, deep down she was just a girl with some serious issues. I'd walked away from her once and her father turned her into a killer. I wasn't going to walk away from her again.

Lila settled our hotel bill and we left for the train station, careful not to draw attention to ourselves now that we were out in public.

Our train was already boarding when we arrived, so we didn't have to wait long before embarking for Perth. I made sure to grab us seats near the door just in case we needed to make a quick escape. There were only a handful of people in the carriage we had chosen, none of whom paid us any attention when we took our seats.

"Hungry?" Lila asked as we rolled out of the station.

"A little," I admitted.

"Here." She reached into her bag and pulled out a plastic-wrapped Danish. "I grabbed a couple from the hotel before we left."

"Thanks." I gave her a small smile and ate the sugary pastry.

We sat in companionable silence as the highland countryside passed us by, the rustle of the train soothing my nerves. The further we got away from Aiden, the better. It would be much harder to track us now that we'd shaken our Magical trail. So long as we could keep under the radar and not use Magic, we'd be safe.

I looked to my left at Lila. She twirled the slender silver ring around her finger nervously.

"You alright?" I whispered.

She looked at me and stopped her fiddling. "Fine why?" she asked.

"You've spent the last thirty minutes polishing the inside of that ring with your finger." I nodded toward her hands, now sitting still in her lap. "Something's bothering you."

A nervous smile tugged at her lips and she turned toward me. "I still can't believe my father was planning to bring Morgana back all this time." She kept her voice just above a whisper.

The other passengers weren't paying any attention to us, but it was always best to be cautious.

"I'm sorry," I replied with as much sincerity as I could muster.

"What am I supposed to do now? I left everything..." she said before trailing off with a weak shrug.

"Now you start over." I placed my hand on hers.

"Right. Start over. With you?" Her big blue eyes looked up at me as she laced her fingers through mine.

"Lila-"

"I just... I don't have anyone else." She cut me off. "But you, you've always been there for me." She reached out her hand, her fingers trailing softly across my jaw.

"Lila. I can't." I pulled her hand from my face and shook my head.

She let out a dry, sarcastic laugh and untwined her fingers from mine. "You can't or won't?"

"I won't."

"Because of Violet?" She looked back up at me and I could see the pain of everything she lost in her eyes. Despite everything she's done, my heart still went out to her.

"You're just lost and clinging to something familiar. But I can't be that for you." I looked out the window. Rolling green hills flew past us in a blur.

"You really do love her, don't you?" Her voice was soft, resolved.

Turning my attention back to her, I shrugged.

"I hope she knows how lucky she is to have you in her corner." She smiled, but there was still pain in her eyes.

"I don't know if she'll see it that way." I ran my hand through my hair out of nervous habit.

"Because I'm with you." Her lips pursed together and her eyes crinkled at the corners as she realized just what a mess we were in.

"It's not like there's going to be a welcoming party when they find out I've brought you back with me."

"I know," she said with a sigh. "It's not going to be easy."

"Honestly, they'll probably try to kill you."

She threw her head back against the padded seat and said, "I wouldn't expect anything less from the Maxwell's."

"I promise I'll do what I can, though. But you've got your work cut out for you, kid." I tapped her knee with my fist.

"Maybe it'd be best if we went our separate ways once we get to the states."

I cocked my head to the side. "That's not going to happen."

"Because you don't trust me?" She looked up at me from under her lashes.

"What do you think?" My body swayed to the motion of the train.

"I guess I can understand that," she shrugged.

"Lila, I get that you thought you were doing the right thing, but you tried to kill Violet, twice. I can't pretend that didn't happen," I explained.

"I know. And I get it. But I want you to know that from here on out, I'm on your side no matter what."

I gave her a smile, but my heart wasn't in it. I wanted to believe her, but after everything we'd been through over the years, I knew how strong of an influence her father had on her. She might mean it at the moment, but there was no way I would let my guard down around her.

We spent the rest of the train ride in silence. There honestly wasn't much more to say. Lila had helped me escape from Avalon, but now she was at my mercy.

We arrived in Perth and found a hotel with vacancies that overlooked the River Tay. I was anxious to get back to Pismo, but I couldn't begrudge a little R&R. We were both starving by the time we got settled in, so we went to the local market and grabbed a stash of frozen dinners and toiletries to take back to our hotel room. It wasn't ideal, but neither one of us wanted to be out in the open. We may have lost Ian for now, but we had no idea who else might still be looking for us. It was best to stay in our room until the time came to head to Glasgow.

DAY 17

Today was the day. I was finally going to return to Pismo and get back to Violet. We checked out of our hotel and made our way back to the station.

Over the last week, Lila and I had gotten into a comfortable routine and it felt almost like old times. Almost. I was still cautious around her, but I started to realize she could be a valuable asset to us.

The train ride lasted only an hour and twenty minutes, but it felt like an eternity. I fidgeted in my seat like child, I was so anxious to get back to Pismo, to get back to Violet. The train started to slow as we neared the station and my body tensed even more.

"When the train comes to a stop, stay close to me, alright," I said and looked at Lila. She nodded.

The train car rattled slowly into the station and the people around us stood to gather their belongings. I grabbed onto Lila's hand as she slung her bag over her shoulder. The moment the doors opened, I rushed onto the platform, dragging her with me.

Another train departed as we walked up the pathway. The

roar of the wheels on steel gliding out of the station filled the air. The smell of fuel and wet concrete assaulted my nose and brought a thousand memories of days gone by flooding into my head. I had always loved train stations. The hustle and bustle of commuters and tourists rushing past one another like a choreographed dance timed perfectly to the departure of each train.

But now was not the time to reminisce. We were here for one thing and one thing only, a way back to Pismo.

"Come on, we have to be quick about this," I said and walked toward the exit with purpose. Lila jogged to keep up with me.

I put my ticket into the turn style and the barrier opened up for me to pass into the station. Lila did the same next to me and we followed the overhead signs directing us to the street.

I had looked up directions from this station to Central Station while we were still in Perth and memorized our route. Exiting the building with Lila in tow, we headed south toward west George Street. I estimated it would only take about six minutes to walk from one station to the next, but I was determined to move faster than the average tourist.

It had been years since I was last in Glasgow and I wished I could take my time and enjoy the sights. The entire city was an exquisite mixture of stone and metal, something I'd always admired about the flourishing city.

"Almost there," I called back to Lila as we turned left onto Buchanan Street, which just so happened to be the main stretch of shops in Glasgow and completely blocked off from cars. I'd chosen this route in the hopes of blending in with the tourist and shoppers. Bagpipes screeched to life somewhere further down the promenade, no doubt a street performer trying to make some extra cash.

I inhaled deeply as we passed a *Starbucks*. The only thing better than the smell of fresh-brewed coffee was the first sip of a dark roast.

"The station is just up ahead," I said as we quickly made our way down Gordon Street.

When the station came into view, we slowed to a walk and I pulled Lila across the street, searching the crowd for anything that looked suspicious.

"Looks like the coast is clear." I grabbed her hand and pulled her toward the train station. Dodging taxis and commuters, we slipped through the side entrance closest to the drop location.

We passed a few shops and restaurants where waiting passengers milled about until their time to leave arrived.

"Alright, you wait out here," I said as we walked up to the coffee shop next to the restroom entrance.

"What, no way."

"I'm going into the men's restroom. You can't exactly follow me."

"Fine, I'll look out for any trouble. But if you're not out of there in two minutes, I'm going in after you."

I nodded and walked through the archway and down the stairs leading to the restrooms and showers. I dug the required thirty pence out of my pocket and paid the turn style to let me enter.

One of the stalls was occupied and another gentleman stood before the sink washing his hands. I entered the middle stall as planned and waved my hand across the wall behind the toilet. A hidden panel raised from the otherwise smooth surface and I reached forward to open it.

It was empty. I stared in disbelief at the vacant space. Malcolm had never been late or unable to deliver before. Something must be wrong.

Realizing a moment too late that it was much too quiet for a public restroom. I turned to leave the stall, but the door fell in on me. Crawling under the wall of the empty stall next to me, I was able to make it into the main restroom before that door fell in as well.

Two men stood in front of me. One held the envelope containing our fake passports and money to get us home. The other stood in a fighting stance. He was clearly the one knocking-in the stall doors.

"Looking for something, Mr. Maxwell?" the man holding the envelope said with a thick Scottish accent.

"Just hand it over. I don't want any trouble," I said, trying to sound threatening but cautious.

"I'm afraid I can't do that. We've got orders, ye see." He turned away from me to head up the stairs. "Take care of him."

The other guy attacked without a second thought. I ducked as his fist came at me and immediately went into a defensive stance. He swung at me again and again as the other guy made off with our envelope.

I couldn't let him get away, I tapped into my Magic, raised my shield and then summoned enough energy to knock my punch happy friend out without killing him. A wave of Magic pulsed off of me and he flew back into the sinks and collapsed to the floor.

Running past his crumpled body, I pushed through the turn style and saw the bulky Scot with our envelope start up the stairs.

"Lila!" I yelled as something hit me square in the back and knocked me over. A heavy boot kicked me in the ribs and I felt a few crack.

"Ye think a little Magic is enough to knock me out?" asked the man I thought I'd taken care of.

I groaned as I stood up and muttered, "It should've been."

"Try again," he said, swinging his leg out and kicking my legs out from under me. Falling like a bag of potatoes, I hit the tile floor with an audible *thud* and he pinned me down. This guy was pure muscle. I was strong, but not strong enough to beat him physically.

He raised his arm to punch me.

"Tardi," I said, and everything around me slowed. His fist moved toward me at a glacial pace, and his face froze in an angry snarl as he hovered above me.

I was stuck in slow motion as well, so all I could do was get my shield up in time not to be punched. It wasn't the best spell to use, but it typically took your attacker off guard.

I could feel my shield slowly materializing around me. A bead of sweat on my attacker balanced perfectly on his brow, moving so slowly my eyes couldn't track its progress. I began to turn my head as fast as I could toward the stairs.

The other man running off with my envelope was also caught in the spell and ran in slow motion up the stairs. His foot hovering between steps in mid-air.

My eyes began to burn and I blinked. Just like that, the spell broke. The man with the envelope's foot hit the next step and my attacker's fist bounced off my shield at a normal speed again.

"Going somewhere?" Lila's smooth voice echoed down the staircase as the burly man with our paperwork flew over my head and crashed into the wall.

My assailant turned his attention off of me for a split second and I took full advantage.

Summoning an Arcane spell, I let the Magic pulse out of me like a shock wave. The spell hit both men, throwing them like rag dolls. They crumpled to the tiled floor in a heap and before either one of them could stand back up, I threw a stunning orb at them to make sure they wouldn't be following us anytime soon.

Lila came running down the stairs as I grabbed the thick manila envelope from the floor.

"Let's get out of here," I said before she was halfway down the steps.

Turning on her heel, she went back the way she'd come. Following behind her, I let the warmth of my healing ability course through me and heal my broken ribs. There weren't enough words to describe how good it felt to have my Magic back.

I took the stairs two at a time and reached the top just behind Lila.

"What the hell happened down there?"

"They were waiting for me. Somehow they knew we'd be here," I explained.

"Do you think Malcolm sold you out?"

"If he did, he didn't do it willingly."

"They'll send backup now that they know where we are." Lila frowned and gave me a grave look.

"I know," I said and held up the envelope. "But we're getting out of here." I smiled and for the first time in weeks, I felt the weight on my chest lift ever so slightly. I was going home, to my family and to Violet.

TEMPEST: ROBERT'S JOURNAL

Dive into Robert's Journal and you'll get to see what his world was like before Violet ever stepped into his life and changed him forever.

Find out what happened to Brett's first love in college.

Watch as Robert learns how to control his Magic.

And learn more about his relationship with Lila.

Sign up to my mailing list to get a FREE copy of Tempest!

http://allisonsipe.com/avalon

THANK YOU!

I hope you enjoyed *Avalon.* Robert was a lot of fun to explore in this Novella and it's such been a privilege to share his story with you. I'm sure you're wondering what happened next and what kind of havoc Morgana is going to bring down on them all!

Well, you're in luck! On the next page you can read the first two chapter of Trivium, or you can go ahead and buy the next book at your favorite retailer or directly from me on my website, allisonsipe.com

I love to hear from my fans, so please feel free to email me any questions or just drop me a line and say hello on my website, allisonsipe.com And again, thank you for taking this journey with Violet and Robert!

Until next time, Embrace Your Magic!

INTRODUCING TRIVIUM

The third installment in the series is here!
Enjoy a free sample on the next page and pick up your copy
today!

CHAPTER 1

His fist barely missed my face as I ducked out of the way and jumped into a defensive stance. He came at me again and I swung around and kicked toward the center of his chest. Without skipping a beat, he grabbed me by the ankle and pulled me off my feet. I hit the ground with an audible grunt as the wind escaped my lungs.

"That was better, but you need to make sure you have a clean shot or you'll just end up on your ass every time," Jake instructed.

"No kidding," I said, pushing myself off the blue padded mats and rubbing my butt and thigh. "Let's go one more round." I wiped the sweat off my brow with my forearm, doing my best to keep my panting in check.

The sun had long since taken its plunge beyond the horizon and still, it was unseasonably warm. The heat combined with the humidity made my skin slick with sweat and forced me to shower twice a day.

"Alright, when you're ready," he said, jogging in place as if training me wasn't enough of a work out for him.

I grabbed a sip of water and when I was ready I chanced a swing at him while he was unprepared.

He blocked me with his forearm. "Fighting dirty, huh?" he asked, stepping back. "Bring it on, Miss Evans." He motioned with his fingers for me to advance.

I took a deep breath and shot forward, alternating my punches. Left, right, uppercut, right, uppercut, left. He effortlessly blocked all my blows but I kept him on the defense and was able to push forward. Taking another step, I swung around and planted a kick against his chest. He stumbled backward.

"There you go," he said, finding his balance and taking a swing at me. It was my turn to dodge and try to get the upper hand. My forearms were already red and sore, but he kept pushing forward. I ducked into a squatting position and swung out my leg, catching his feet and bringing him to the mat.

Applause came from behind us and catch my attention. Annabel and Brett stood watching us from the patio.

"It's about time someone put my husband in his place," Annabel laughed, waving playfully at Jake.

"You're really coming along, kiddo," Jake said from the mats, resting on his elbows.

"It's all those cardio kickboxing classes I used to take," I replied, reaching down to help him up.

"He's right, you're doing great," Brett said, stepping toward us.

"I'm motivated. I just wish my Magic was coming along as quickly as my self-defense."

Jake pat my shoulder as he stood. "Magic takes time and a lot of practice, but you'll get there."

"I hope so," I sighed. I had the ability to see the past, present, and future but I still couldn't get a solid read on where Robert was or what had happened to him and it was slowly driving me insane.

As a small measure of self-preservation, I threw myself into training. The hour or so I spent sparring with Jake every day was the only time Robert wasn't on my mind. When fists and legs are flying at you, it's hard to think about anything else.

"So what are you ladies up to?" Jake asked.

"Actually, I came out to talk to you," Brett said. She raised her eyebrows and tilted her head. Jake nodded slightly, and if I wasn't watching him I wouldn't have noticed.

"And I just wanted to grab a quick kiss before heading out," Annabel stood up on her tiptoes to steal a peck.

"You're going somewhere?" Jake asked Annabel.

"Just need to run to the store, I'll be back before you know it," she said.

"Alright, see you in a bit." Jake smiled down at her and tapped her backside before she orbed out of sight.

Another careful lie. Annabel was doing some research for me in secret. She was the only one I'd opened up to about my parents besides Robert and she was helping me search for answers. Her ability to orb in and out of hard to reach places always proved useful.

Annabel was also the only one on my side about Robert, which made her that much easier to be around and open up to. Sure, Jake wanted his brother back and believed Robert was still on our side, but he wasn't in a rush to look for him either. I think Brett was really starting to wear him down. And who could blame him, with each day that passed, it was getting easier to believe that Robert was never coming back.

"Let's call it for tonight. We can practice more tomorrow," Jake concluded, wiping a towel across his face.

"Sounds good. Aunt Beth should be here soon to work on my Magic anyway," I agreed, and wiped my own sweat off of my forehead with the end of my shirt.

Over the last few weeks, I had started getting used to spending most of my time at the Maxwell estate. Brett and Annabel had really helped me after the battle at Pacifica Pier, and Jake was becoming more and more like a brother to me. Once I recovered from my near drowning, he began meticulously training me in the art of self-defense, while everyone else was helping me hone my magic.

I thought about how proud Robert would be of the progress I've made and my heart ached that he wasn't here to see it. He was my first introduction to Magic and I'd fought him every step of the way. If only he could see how much I'd embraced the Magical world in the weeks since he'd been missing.

Leaving the changing room, I walked over to the pool and dove in. The cool water washing over my body was refreshing after a rigorous session of training. I did a couple laps, enjoying the feel of the water on my skin, and then rolled over and relaxed, floating aimlessly around the pool.

I moved my arms back and forth, creating ripples across the water as the rhythmic sloshing relaxed my mind. The stars above twinkled like diamonds against the black velvet of the sky. Propelling myself through the water, gently kicking my feet and using my arms to steer, I admired the cosmos.

My Magic squirmed inside me, begging for release as my thoughts wandered back to Robert. I wished I could see if he had betrayed us or not, I wished I could see if he was okay. The power inside of me hummed just beneath the surface, ready and waiting. There was something about the water that made my Magic flare up stronger and more robust than any other time. I always tried to reach out to Robert while I was in the water, hoping that extra boost would allow me to get a clear picture of him.

Taking a deep breath, I swished my hair back and forth, letting the strands float across my shoulders like seaweed. Magic soared inside me as I thought about the last time Robert and I were alone together and a warm feeling began to spread through my torso.

The stars swirled above me like Van Goth's, *Starry Night* as a vision took hold.

Robert was fast asleep on a thin cotton mattress. He looked peaceful as his chest rose and fell with each gentle breath. Quiet footsteps made their way down the hall and I peered through the bars to see who it might be.

It was Lila. She gazed over her shoulder as if to make sure the coast was clear and then waved her hand over the locked bars. They slid open with ease and she quietly walked over to where Robert was sleeping.

Oh god, what was she going to do to him, I thought.

"Robert, wake up," Lila whispered into his ear. She gently shook him until he opened his eyes.

He rolled over languidly and looked up at the woman hovering over him. His eyes widened at the sight of her and he jumped to his feet, saying, "What, what is it. What's wrong?"

"We have to go." She looked over her shoulder. "Now."

"We?" he asked, rubbing the sleep from his eyes.

"I promise I'll explain later, but we need to go." She held out her hand for Robert to grab, her expression deadly serious.

Colors and shapes swirled around me as the scene changed again and Robert and Lila were standing near the ruins of a castle arguing.

Before I could get a good look at the scenery, my vision went dark and a hotel room rose around me. Lila walked out of the bathroom, letting the yellow light flood the room with a healthy glow. She wore a towel wrapped around her and quietly padded across the carpet on tiptoes.

I was able to look around and spotted Robert asleep on the oversized bed. My vision crossed the room to Robert's prone form and I watched him sleep. The light from the bathroom touched his face, highlighting the dark circles under his eyes and stubble around his jaw. A hot branding iron seared through my heart and angry tears filled my eyes. How could he be with Lila after she tried to kill me?

Lila switched off the bathroom light and the room plunged into darkness.

CHAPTER 2

An hour later, Annabel orbed us into my living room. I didn't spend much time at home anymore. It was too lonely without Robert.

I chided myself at the thought of how quickly he'd become a fixture in my life. When he was here it felt safe, comfortable, like a home should. But without him, it was cold and lonely.

Brett had tried to convince me to stay at the estate. They had plenty of empty bedrooms, but I didn't want to give up every last shred of my old life. Instead, the Maxwells took turns staying with me, insisting that I couldn't be left alone.

"Violet, are you alright?" Annabel asked, eyeing me as I dropped to the couch in a heap of sore muscles.

"Fine. Why?"

"Jake told me the history behind Robert and Lila." Her eyes drifted around the room. "He said you might need someone to talk to."

"Something doesn't add up," I ignored her mention of Robert and Lila's past relationship. "Why take Robert on the beach and then help him escape?"

It took all of me not to jump to conclusions since my heart

wanted to scream at the thought of him trusting her, after everything she'd put me through.

"Do you want to punch something?" Annabel asked. She half smiled and shrugged.

I laughed and said, "No, I'm fine. I just don't get how he can align himself with her, you know?"

"What do you mean? You don't think he's just using her to escape?" Annabel crossed her arms, waiting for more of an explanation.

Turning to face her, I took a deep breath and closed my eyes before answering. Annabel and I had gotten close over the past month and I was pretty sure I could trust her not to say anything. But still, I was worried.

"Violet, you've got to tell me what's going on. You can't keep everything in all the time," she pleaded as she sat down next to me and picked up my hands in hers.

"I just don't know what to make of it, and I don't want to add any more fuel to the Robert fire," I reasoned.

Annabel chuckled. "I'm not Brett. I won't gather a hunting party based on one little vision."

I thought about it for a moment and then leaned against the back of the couch. "After they escaped, I saw them together in a hotel room," I began.

"Like, *together*, together?" she asked suggestively, her eyebrows almost meeting her hairline.

"No, nothing like that. He was sleeping and she had just gotten out of the shower."

Annabel's eyes shifted to the side and she bit the inside of her cheek. "Do you think he's on her side now?"

"I don't know." Even to my own ears, my voice sounded flat. "I only got short flashes of them, not much to go on." I ran my hand through my hair. "How can he be so relaxed around her after…" I trailed off and kept my eyes on the ground, unable to meet Annabel's gaze. "I know, it doesn't look good."

"That doesn't mean they're in cahoots." Annabel tried to sound optimistic but I could tell it was getting harder and harder for her to ignore the facts.

"Do you think there could be an explanation for why he's with her that doesn't lead to him being a traitor?" I asked.

"I don't know. Maybe Brett's right. I mean, he is fraternizing with the woman who tried to kill you," Annabel said. She looked no more eager than I to think over the possibility of Robert being a traitor.

"There's clearly some level of trust between them. If there wasn't he wouldn't have been fast asleep with her in the same room," I concluded.

Annabel shifted, clearly uncomfortable. She had to know I was right, but we both wanted to believe that Robert would come home and still be on our side.

"You may have the gift of Sight, but not everything you see comes with an explanation. What does your gut tell you?" she asked.

I huffed, my cheeks puffing out, and said, "I don't know if it's my gut or my heart, but something feels wrong about all of this. The pieces just don't add up."

"Alright, so until we know more, I say we cautiously hold onto hope."

"Thanks, Annabel." I gave her hands a gentle squeeze.

Pushing off the couch, I made my way into the kitchen and opened the refrigerator. I was parched and the condo was still stuffy despite leaving the windows open all day. The carafe of sweet tea I'd made yesterday would be the perfect antidote for this hot, sticky weather.

"Want some?" I asked, holding up the pitcher so Annabel could see it from the living room.

"I'm good, I can't have caffeine at night," she said, waving me off.

"I have to say, it's nice being able to talk to someone I don't have to lie through my teeth to." I took a sip of the sugary iced tea.

"You get used to it." Annabel shrugged and flipped through the book I'd left on the coffee table.

"I know. That's what everyone keeps saying. It's just been hard, not being able to talk to the people I care about."

"You mean Becky?"

I nodded. I hadn't seen Becky in a couple weeks and it was really taking its toll on both of us. Sure, we talked on the phone every couple of days, but I'd been so focused on my physical and Magical training that I'd been too drained to have a fake conversation with my best friend.

"Have you ever thought about telling her the truth?" Annabel asked.

"Robert would die if he heard you say that," I said, choking on a large gulp.

"Robert's always had a stick up his ass about secrecy and rules." She rolled her eyes and dismissed the idea with a wave of her hand. "There was this one time, Jake and I orbed into his place overseas. He had a few people over playing cards or something and when we popped into the room, he literally flipped the entire table." She snickered. "Apparently not everyone was Magical at the game and we got chewed out big time."

"How did he explain you materializing out of thin air?"

She shrugged and said, "He didn't. Everyone had been drinking and just assumed that Jake and I had come from the other room. They were more surprised by Robert's sudden outburst than anything else."

I shook my head and chuckled at the thought of Robert causing a scene over Annabel flaunting the rules.

Annabel waved her hand dismissively. "People don't believe in Magic. So when they see something unexplainable, they find a way to explain it with logic. Robert's just too old school sometimes."

"He kind of is, isn't he?" I mused.

It was nice being able to joke about him and reminisce. Annabel was great in that way. I think that's why I gravitated toward her more than anyone else. With Annabel, the pain of losing Robert didn't hurt as much.

"By the dreamy look in your eyes, I'd say you like that about him," Annabel noted, eyeing me as a secretive smile spread across her face.

"Anyway, back to telling the truth," I urged.

"Changing the subject." She pursed her lips. "Did I hit a nerve?"

I nudged her leg and said, "I don't think I could drag Becky into all this," I mustered on, determined not to talk about my feelings for Robert. "Every time I turn around, someone's trying to kill me. I don't want to put her in harm's way."

Annabel sighed and said, "I hate to break this to you, but you can't protect everyone. You have to let people make their own choices once they have all the facts."

"I don't know. I just think keeping Magic a secret is better for everyone."

"Morgana's back from the dead and she'll be amassing an army to take over the Magical world. Do you really think that's going to stay under the radar?"

"That's just one more reason not to tell Becky." I closed my eyes and rubbed the bridge of my nose. "Morgana is going to rain hell down on us. I don't want my friend getting caught up in the middle if I can help it."

Annabel raised her hands in surrender. "Alright, but for the record, I think having her in the know would help you more than you think."

"Duly noted." I tapped her on the knee and stood. "I'm going to hop in the shower and get to bed. Your husband exhausted me."

"Some women might take that the wrong way." She gave me a teasing grin.

I rolled my eyes. "You know what I mean."

"As a matter of fact, I do. Jake can be rigorous with his training." Annabel wiggled her eyebrows suggestively.

I shook my head and laughed. "Alright, see you in the morning."

Annabel stretched out on the couch and turned on the T.V. Unlike myself, she was a night owl and would no doubt be up for another few hours binge-watching something on Netflix.

"Night," she called after me, already searching through the catalog of movies and TV shows.

I turned on the shower and ducked under the faucet while the water was still cool, letting the artificial rain wash away the sweat and chlorine from the day's activities. As I rinsed off, I could feel my muscles start to relax. Jake really was kicking my ass, but I couldn't complain. I'd rather be ready for a fight than a helpless damsel in distress. After Pacifica Pier, I never wanted to feel helpless like that again.

As the water warmed up, I let it stream down my neck and shoulders, loosening up the tension of the day. I wish I could say my training was responsible for the tightness in my shoulders, but it wasn't. Constantly worrying about Robert, Aiden and now Morgana was wreaking havoc on my upper back and my nightly shower was my only reprieve.

With my eyes closed and the warm water at the base of my neck, I could feel a vision tingling just under the surface of my Magic. Dropping my walls, I let the vision take me.

Annabel was chained to a wall, grime and blood staining her skin as she screamed. A flash of green light shot from the shadows and her body went limp. Running toward her, the vision began to fade. As I reached her, a deep, chuckle echoed through my bones.

The image of Annabel was quickly replaced by the back of my eyelids. Heart racing, dread pooled in the pit of my stomach as water cascaded off of me. Swinging the faucet into the off position, I jumped out of the shower and ran down the hall, barely getting a towel around me as I stormed into the living room.

Annabel laid on the couch, her head propped up on a pile of pillows while Matt Damon jumped off of a building on the screen in front of her.

Letting out the breath I'd been holding, Annabel turned to look at me.

"Everything okay? She asked.

Unable to meet her eyes I said, "yeah, just grabbing a glass of water." I padded across the carpet to the kitchen, trying my best to act normal.

My aunt had taught me that the future can always shift and change based on free will. Sharing what we see with someone can have a direct influence on the vision and in some cases, the knowledge can be the catalysts that creates the future we've seen. Until I had more to go on, there was no way I could tell Annabel anything. For now, she was safe and that's all that mattered.

"Night," I said, taking my glass of water with me to bed.

"Night," Annabel replied, her eyes stayed glued to the T.V.

Throwing on a pair of shorts and a t-shirt, I jumped into bed. With the soothing effects of my shower long gone, I picked up the journal Robert had given to me off the night-stand. Reading William's words helped me get to sleep some-times. Cracking open to a random page, William's handwriting sprawled out in tiny neat letters and I began to read.

13 May 1783

My heart is heavy after leaving Constance this morning, and not with sorrow but worry. Her betrothed appears to have a connection with Le Fay. How a person could choose to align themselves with Le Fay, I'll never know. Even now, drawing out each letter of their moniker makes me sick. To join them would surely be the death of one's soul.

My conscience pulls at me like a bridle in the mouth of a horse. I feel it is my duty to report him, no matter how small his involvement may be.

But alas, fear of betraying my promise to Constance I shall say nothing as of yet. My only worry is that she'll get hurt or even killed if we wait too long. How can I keep her safe when I've been banished back to the shadows?

Letting the journal fall onto my lap, I stared at the ceiling.

Le Fay? Who the hell were they? I thought. I couldn't help but wonder if Robert knew anything about them. He was always the one with all the answers. How was I supposed to navigate this world without him?

I replaced the journal on the nightstand, turned off the light and rolled over on my side. Normally it was easy to fall asleep after reading through William's journal. But the vision of Annabel had left me paranoid about the future and William's words nagged at me as the name, Le Fay danced around in my head. My eyes darted around the room, as I thought about how quickly everything was changing again. There was still so much more I didn't know about the Magical world.

My chest filled with doubt and before I could go down the rabbit hole of self-pity and anxiety, I pictured the ocean. The dark blue water, the golden sand. The feel of the cool breeze on my skin as a wave crashed on the shore. The images floating around my head did wonders to combat the darkness rising inside of me and slowly, I fell asleep.

Visions of Robert and Lila infiltrated my dreams. They boarded a train and lush green countryside rushed past them. They arrived in a bustling city, the buildings a mix of stone and steal. I watched them run across cobblestone streets and duck into a busy train station. Hundreds of nameless faces rushing passed them as Robert pulled Lila behind him. And last but not least, I saw the name of a hotel here in Pismo and a room number: 324.

My eyes shot open and I stared at the ceiling with a heavy heart and I knew without a doubt, he was back. Still exhausted, I looked at the clock on the nightstand. I'd barely slept four hours. Groaning, I rolled over, wishing to fall back asleep.

I knew I was going to have to face him, but the thought of seeing him with Lila hurt more than I cared to admit. My heart didn't know how to reconcile what I felt for him now that he had returned to Pismo with the woman who had tried to kill me. It didn't matter that they had a history. He was supposed to protect me, to keep me safe, not harbor the woman who wanted me dead.

Closing my eyes, I let myself relive every moment with Robert. Falling asleep on his warm chest, his smile when I told him I wanted to learn how to use my Magic. A tear rolled down my cheek as I imagined his arms around me, his lips on mine and the warmth of his body pressed against me. I let myself feel the comfort of him one last time, and then I boxed him up and hid him in the darkest corner of my heart.

The path ahead wasn't going to be easy and I couldn't let my feelings for Robert get in the way. My mission was to wake The Lady, and if Robert and Lila were there to stop me, I'd make sure neither of them ever saw the light of day again.

Steeling my nerves for what had to be done, I got out of bed and got dressed. I wanted to meet Robert alone, find out what he was up to before Brett and the others jumped to any conclusions.

Sneaking out of the house came easy after my physical training, and Annabel remained fast asleep. I went out through my bedroom sliding door, grabbed my bike and rode off into the early morning light to find out where Robert's loyalties truly lay.

Parking my single speed out front, I walked nervously into

the lobby of the Sandcastle Inn. The signs led me to the elevator and I took it up to the third floor. The Magic inside me kicked up a notch as if it knew Robert was close by. As the elevator slowly moved between floors, my heart battered against my ribcage and Magic crackled on my fingertips. My hands shook as I tried to regain control of the power coursing through me.

The silence of the hotel made the prominent *ding* of the elevator seem much more menacing. The doors slid open and I stood, motionless, staring at the wall across from me. Chills ran down my entire body as an image of Robert and Lila sleeping peacefully flashed across my eyes.

As the door began to close, I put my arm out, stopping them, then turned left down the hall. My eyes shifted back and forth as room numbers passed me by: *312, 313, 314, 316.*

At the far end of the hall, I found room number 324, and raised my hand to knock, hesitating for a moment. Sucking in a breath and steeling my nerves, my knuckled banged on the door. I waited a second but not a sound came from the other side. Knocking again, I banged my closed fist against the pristine white door. Within a few seconds I could hear the distinct sounds of whispers and knew I had caught them off guard.

The door slowly cracked open and a disheveled-looking Robert stood in front of me.

"Violet?" he said, exhaling with sleepy eyes.

A smile spread across my face at the sound of his voice. Everything I'd tried to bury, to extinguish inside me came to life at the sight of him. I missed him so desperately, his warmth, his comfort. I wanted to reach out to him, touch his face and feel his skin. I tried to move toward him but my feet stayed rooted to the ground. The rush of seeing him again had taken over, but my subconscious still held onto the real reason I was here.

"It's really you," he said and took a cautious step toward me.

"It is," I said, pushing everything I felt for him back into the box I'd created.

A smile blossomed on his face. "It's such a relief to see you with my own eyes." He pulled the door open wider and allowed me to enter.

Standing with my back against the wall, I watched him retreat into the room. My heart reached out to him but he was no longer the Robert I once knew. Lila had taken him and had somehow made him believe he could trust her.

Their room was large, even by hotel standards, but I shouldn't have expected anything less. Passing a spacious kitchen on my right, I slowly moved into the living room. A door to what I assumed was the bedroom remained closed and the light from a TV flashed under the door.

"How are you?" Robert asked, watching me cautiously as if I was a snake ready to strike.

The sound of his voice tugged at my heart and threatened my resolve. I needed to get away from him and finish what I came here to do.

"Robert, who's at the–" a soft voice came from the doorway just to my right.

I turned toward the woman's voice and saw her, Lila. My resolve slammed into me and any notion of Robert fled my mind as blood boiled under my skin.

"How did you know where to find us?" Lila asked. She stared at me in complete disbelief.

"I have my tricks," I answered with a wicked smile. I enjoyed seeing the uncertainty in her eyes.

Raising my hand, my fingertips ached to release the Magic building inside of me. She deserved to die after what she put me through.

"No!" Robert yelled, and put himself between Lila and me. "Violet, don't. It's not her fault."

"Not her fault?" I narrowed my eyes on him. "She tried to kill me." Magic flared in my heart, ready to strike the second he let his guard down.

"Please, just let me explain," Robert pleaded.

"There's nothing to explain."

He raised his arms in defense. "Violet, let's talk this out."

"I will go through you if I have to." I held his gaze, daring him to challenge me.

"This isn't who you are." Robert took a step toward me as Lila recomposed herself and moved into a defensive stance.

"Don't you dare try and tell me who I am! You come back here with *her* and think you can just pick up where you left off?" I demanded, my voice laced with venom. All the hurt, frustration and anger I held in my heart burst to the surface.

"I knew it wasn't going to be easy coming back here with Lila, but I know I can get you to understand if you just hear me out," Robert reasoned and took another step toward me. His eyes held mine and the warmth I'd missed so much started rising within me.

I threw up my shield, blocking him from coming any closer. But what I felt wasn't something I could block out. My heart echoed with each step he took, making my Magic leap in excitement as it recognized its counterpart in his soul. Nothing could have prepared me for this. I was used to how my Magic felt, but this was different. This was powerful in a way I'd never felt before. Standing frozen behind my shield, I tried to fight for control.

His features matched my anxiety and I wondered if he was feeling the same Magical pull I was.

"Just let me explain before you do anything rash," Robert pleaded.

Looking past Robert to Lila, I watched her slowly raise her hands in surrender. I could still feel Robert's warmth mingling with the Magic inside me, but I was able to concentrate just enough to glance at Lila's future.

Flashes of her filled my vision. She sat on the hotel bed, crying. As I moved closer, she wiped the tears from her eyes and huffed loudly. "It's going to be okay, Lila," she told herself.

The room swirled around me and Robert and Lila sat in the front seats of his Tesla. He held her hand reassuringly and said, "We're going to make it through this."

"How?" she asked, keeping her eyes trained on the windshield.

Robert's lips pressed into a hard line and he said nothing.

"They all hate me. I don't belong here," Lila continued.

"Don't let Brett get to you. She's difficult even on her best days, you know that," Robert said.

"It's not just her. Violet looks like she's plotting a million ways to kill me." Lila looked at him from under her lashes, eyes still blurry with tears.

"You don't have to worry about Violet. She would never purposely hurt someone."

"You underestimate her." Lila cracked a small smile. "But I guess you always do see the best in the people you love."

Robert's worried expression came back into view and Lila watched me anxiously. I wasn't sure how I felt about seeing Lila in a vulnerable state but I knew, for the moment at least, she wasn't a threat.

Letting my shield drop, I lowered my hand and nodded in agreement that I wouldn't attack.

"Thank you," Robert said, reaching out to touch me but dropped his hand at the last second. He took a step back and I let out the breath I hadn't realized I'd been holding.

"Alright, go ahead and try to explain why you've allied yourself with *her*," I spat.

"I should probably apologize," Lila noted, stepping forward.

I shot her a look that should have killed her on the spot.

"Violet, she's on our side now," Robert insisted. "Once she found out the truth she helped me escape and-"

"You wouldn't have needed help escaping if it wasn't for her," I pointed out.

"Look, I was just taking orders," Lila said, taking another step toward me.

"So what? You don't think twice when you're ordered to kill someone?" I matched her step. I wasn't helpless anymore and I was going to knock her through the wall if she didn't back off.

"I was told you were a threat to my family, to the Magical world. As far as I knew, you were going to kill us all. What would you do in that situation?" she yelled.

My hatred toward her fueled the Magic inside me. How could I honestly sit here and have a conversation with this woman?

"Did you ever bother to think for yourself?" I yelled back. Anger pushed me forward and my Magic ached to be used.

"Violet, calm down," Robert urged.

"Don't," I snapped at Robert and moved closer to Lila. "And don't pretend you and Ian didn't enjoy trying to kill me. You may be able to fool him." I motioned in Robert's direction. "But I was there, and you loved every torturous minute." Something inside me snapped and a wall of energy flew off me, tossing Lila across the room.

Lila bounced to her feet in a second, hot white light surrounding her fingers. Robert quickly moved between us and grabbed her by the shoulders. "Don't do this," he demanded. "We knew this wasn't going to be easy."

"Fine," Lila seethed and threw the orb of energy she wielded against the back of the couch.

Robert let out a sigh of relief and his shoulders relaxed ever so slightly.

"I think it'd be best if I left you two alone," Lila said and nodded curtly at Robert. Something private passed between them and I felt a pang of jealousy deep in my stomach.

Lila walked to the door and paused as she grabbed her jacket. "I really do hope we can move past this, Violet," she said.

"Not likely," I replied without turning to look at her. I heard the door close behind me and suddenly I was very aware that I was alone in a hotel room with Robert.

"Will you please sit down and let me tell you everything?" he said, motioning toward the couch in the small living room.

"There's nothing to say, Robert. You've made your choice. I don't care how well she plays the part, I will never trust her." I turned away from him and walked to the door as well.

I had to get out of there before my resolve cracked. With Lila gone, my anger began to subside and I couldn't afford to let Robert break through even the slightest bit, so long as he was close to her.

"Violet, wait." He grabbed my hand as I walked away.

His touch was like an electric shock and I froze mid-step.

"What?" I barked.

"I know you must hate me." He pulled at my hand, turning me to face him. "But you have to know that I would never put you in harm's way. Lila is a lost and lonely soul, always has been. I couldn't just leave her with Aiden. He would have killed her."

"Maybe she deserves to die." I pulled my hand free of his and tried to steel my nerves.

"You don't mean that." He shook his head and looked away from me.

"You sure about that? You have no idea what she put me through. What you put me through. I've been worried sick about you, whether you're alive, dead, being tortured. Instead, I find you all cozy and lounging around with the enemy."

"For God's sake, Violet. You want the truth, then open your eyes and *see* for yourself." He grabbed my wrist and our Magic exploded between us with such force it knocked the breath out of me.

My vision swirled and a small, dank chamber materialized around me.

Moonlight pooled on the floor at my feet and an older woman sat on the edge of her bed.

"Hello, Violet," she said, slowly raising her head to look at me.

"You, you can see me?" I asked, taking a hesitant step forward. No one in any of my visions had been able to see me before.

"Yes, I can. I've been waiting for Robert to get back to you."

"Who are you?"

"Who I am is not important. I need you to listen. We don't have much time."

"Okay," I said, hesitantly. This was definitely unexpected.

"They have found a way to modify our ability to see." She gave me a meaningful look. So she was a Soothsayer too. I wondered if all Soothsayers could communicate like this. I'd have to ask my aunt.

"You mean, he can block our visions?" I asked.

"Yes. You must be careful who you trust now more than ever, for you won't be able to see the danger until it's too late."

"Lila?"

A loud bang caught her attention and she looked around anxiously. "I must go now," she said.

"No, wait. What about Lila?"

"Don't blame Robert. He did what he had to, to survive."

"But—"

"Good luck, Waker of The Lady."

Just like that, she disappeared, and Robert's hotel room materialized around me. Looking about, I realized I was on the floor and propped up against the wall. Robert knelt next to me with his hand on my shoulder to steady me.

"You alright?" he asked.

"I'm fine," I said, brushing his hand off of me and pushing myself to my feet.

"You're Magic's come along in my absence."

A sarcastic laugh escaped my throat. "I've been going through the Maxwell Magical boot camp."

"You've been training with Jake and Brett?"

I shrugged. "I wanted to learn how to protect myself so I'd

never end up helpless again." It was so easy falling back into a rhythm with him.

"So can we move past all of this now?" He leaned against the wall, his arms crossed, his eyes searching mine.

As I looked back at him I could hear the old woman's words in my head. *"Don't blame Robert."*

"I don't know if I'll ever be able to really trust you again," I said, sighing and stepping away from him. I did blame him for coming back with Lila. He chose to escape with her. He chose to come back to Pismo with her. And the whole time, he knew what she put me through.

"What did you see?" he asked. The sadness in his eyes almost broke me. I wanted to comfort him, but I wouldn't let myself, I couldn't let myself.

There was no way I would tell him about the Soothsayer who had just hijacked my vision, so instead, I decided to tell him what I saw when I looked into Lila.

"I saw Lila opening up to you, but it's just words, Robert. They mean nothing when you compare them to her actions," I explained, taking another step away from him. "I think you want to see the good in Lila. But just because you want something to be true doesn't mean it is." I shook my head and my heart broke as I took another step away from him.

"I know you don't believe she has any good left in her," he reasoned, closing the gap between us. "But I promise you, Violet, I would never have brought her here if I thought she would try to harm you in any way."

He stopped our bodies inches apart. My heart raced and my lips fell open as I took a ragged breath.

"Robert, I..." he grabbed my arm and my words got stuck in my throat. The heat of his body engulfed me and I tried to take a step back to clear my head but ran into the wall. My back pressed against the cool plaster as Robert inched closer.

"Every day I was away, all I could think about was getting

back here to my family, to you. This isn't exactly how I imagined the reunion would go," Robert lamented.

"Me either," I couldn't help agreeing. A lump formed in my throat and the little box hidden deep inside my heart started to rattle. His eyes caught mine and for a brief moment, I thought he was going to reach out to me.

"I know it won't be easy, but I will earn your trust back. One way or another."

Swallowing the lump in my throat, I managed to find the doorknob and opened the door. "We'll see about that," I said, stepping over the threshold.

"Will you do me one favor?" He followed right behind me and I could feel his breath on my neck. My heart accelerated and I had to fight the urge to turn around and face him.

"Depends."

"I'd like you to tell my family I want to see them. I need to talk to everyone, including you, and I think they'll handle seeing me better if you warn them first."

"I can't promise they'll want to see you."

"I know."

"Alright, I'll tell them."

He took a deep breath, and I could tell he was relieved. "I'll come by the estate later today."

Nodding once, I turned on my heel and left without another word.

The warm early morning air outside the lobby doors hit me like a ton of bricks. I knew I should call Brett or Annabel but I was too furious with Robert to think rationally. Dialing Becky's number, I knew she would let me vent without question.

"Hey, what's up?" Becky answered, her voice crackling as she forced herself to wake up.

"Are you home?" I asked. My heart wouldn't stop racing as I made my way through the exit of the hotel.

"Yeah, is everything alright?"

"Fine. I'll be there in five." I ended the call and hopped onto my bike.

Luckily Becky's place was only a couple miles from the hotel so when I pulled up, she was already standing on the porch waiting for me.

"I thought you might like a warm cup of Joe," she said, handing me a hand painted ceramic mug.

"Thanks." I took a large gulp and the caramel-colored liquid warmed my chest and soothed my broken heart.

"So what's got you all worked up?" she asked, rubbing the sleep from her eyes.

"Robert. He's back in town," I said, trying to keep the emotion out of my voice.

Her eyes widened and her mug froze halfway to her mouth. "How'd you find out?"

"I ran into him and this other woman," I lied. It was easier if Becky believed Robert had left me for someone else. My relationship with Becky had turned into careful truths and white lies. I didn't like it, but there was no way I could tell her there was a whole Magical world right under her nose.

"God, what an ass. What is he even still doing here?" she asked. "I thought he was just supposed to be here for the wedding."

I bit my lip. "I guess he's sticking around now."

"Yeah, well that was all fine and good when he was ogling you, but now he needs to go."

Releasing a heavy-hearted sigh, I closed my eyes and let my mind wander to a simpler time when I was sitting on this very couch with Robert.

"Are you okay?" Becky asked, setting her cup down.

"I just didn't think it'd be that hard to see him again," I admitted, this time a truth.

"You really cared about him, of course it hurts to see him with someone else."

"I just keep wondering if things could have been diff-"

"Don't start playing the 'what if' game," she cut me off.

I ran my hand through my hair. "You should have seen the way he looked at me. His eyes were so full of guilt."

"Don't do that to yourself. You deserve better and you know it."

"I know, it's just complicated."

"No, it's not, it's simple. He's an ass and not worth your time."

I laughed. "Thanks, Beck."

"Always." She smiled and retrieved her cup. We each took a sip of coffee. Becky was still my best friend but there was an awkwardness between us now. Like some part of her knew I was keeping things from her.

"I know things have been different since I've been spending so much time at the Maxwell estate. It's nice to know that some things will always stay the same," I said and kicked her foot with my own.

"You never have to worry about me bailing on you. And besides, Annabel's been trying to help you learn more about your parents. I would never stand in the way of that."

I smiled. Another half-truth. Annabel was helping me, just not in the way Becky thought. It was strange how easy living a lie had become. I used to chide Brett about it, but now I under-stood how necessary it was.

"I know," I said. "I just feel bad that I've been so preoccupied. What's new with you? How's work?"

"Work's been really busy actually." She rubbed the back of her neck.

"Anything juicy?" I asked over the rim of my mug.

She shook her head and said, "You know I can't tell you anything."

"I know, I know." I rolled my eyes. "So how's what's his name?"

She looked at the ceiling and bit her lip.

"Come out with it." I knew she had to be brimming with stories of her latest escapades.

Becky didn't disappoint. She launched into a story about the latest guy she was dating and if I didn't think about it too hard, I could almost pretend we were just two normal women gossiping about the men in our lives. Almost.

Unfortunately, the thought of Robert lingered on my mind in a way I couldn't talk with Becky about. I needed to tell his family he was back in town with Lila, which wasn't going to go over well. I knew Jake would be happy to see his brother alive, but no one would welcome him with open arms once they found out he'd brought Lila back with him.

Today is going to be a long day, I thought as I took another sip of coffee and nodded along to Becky's story.

ACKNOWLEDGMENTS

First and foremost, I must thank my friends and family for their continued support. Writing a book takes a lot of time and effort and without your encouragement and constant text messages asking for the next book, it would be much harder. Thank you so much and I love you all!

David, you have helped me grow as a writer over the last two books and I count my lucky stars that you are my editor. I can't wait to work on the next book with you and continue to make Magic!

I would be remiss if I didn't thank one of my closest friends, Jessica. You have been on this journey with me from the beginning and it makes me so happy to share each and every book with you. Thank you so much for reading every first draft and thank you for letting me always talk to you about the fictional characters living inside my head!

Eric, you gave me the courage to follow my dreams and I will never be able to thank you enough for that. Without Soothsayer, there wouldn't be Avalon. You're support, love and patience keeps me writing! I love you to pieces!

Where would I be with my parent's. They have always pushed me to be the best version of myself and I can't thank them enough for it. Growing up my brother and I watched my parents build an empire of their own and I can only hope to follow in their footsteps. Thank you guys for everything you've done for me over the years and thank you for helping me follow my dreams now!

Lastly, I must thank everyone who read Soothsayer! Your kind words and praise have encouraged me to keep writing and keep telling stories! Thank you, thank you, thank you!

ABOUT THE AUTHOR

Allison Sipe lives in Southern California with her husband and two dogs. She has a degree from California State University Northridge in English Literature and is very proud to have gone to school for something she loves.

When she's not writing or spending hours obsessing over other books with friends, she loves to travel the world, go to Disneyland and look for Magik is ordinary places.

www.allisonsipe.com